HUMAN BEINGS

BY RACHAEL LLEWELLYN

HUMAN BEINGS

A COLLECTION

RACHAEL LLEWELYN

FFF
HORROR

Stories in this collection deal with sensitive topics including sexual assualt, child abuse, and suicide.

Human Beings

Rachael Llewellyn

Published in North America by Foul Fantasy Fiction, an imprint of Bear Hill Publishing.
www.foulfantasyfiction.com
www.bearhillbooks.com

Cover image: SvedOliver/Shutterstock
Cover design © 2021 Bear Hill Publishing

Paperback ISBN 978-1-989071-30-4

Hardcover ISBN 978-1-989071-31-1

Ebook ISBN 978-1-989071-32-8

For Amanda and George, who always have time for something scary

HUMAN BEINGS

HUMAN BEINGS

THE LOVE OF THE RED BEETLE

Once upon a time, there was an unusual little girl. She was neither pretty nor ugly, thin nor fat. She wasn't especially tall. In her class photograph, she never really stood out. She could be that girl sat behind you in your science lesson. Or maybe that girl you see at the back of the bus. But this little girl existed all the same.

The little girl was not openly unusual, but if you were to ask a classmate or teacher to describe her more closely, they would express a complete lack of knowledge.

What colour are her eyes? You might ask.

Brown, the classmate or teacher might answer. Or perhaps they are green? Or maybe blue? I'm not really sure.

You have no idea? You might press. There is quite a big difference between brown or blue, isn't there?

Well, I suppose so, the classmate or teacher might say. But honestly, I've never really thought about it.

That was the standard answer regarding this child and her behaviour. Nobody seemed to have given anything about her very much thought.

What were her parents like, you might wonder? Well, there was a man, or perhaps a woman who picked her up after school. And, her teacher was sure there had been a man and a woman who'd come to parents' evening. What were they like? They wore . . . navy blue coats, the teacher was confident. And the neighbours were sure they had seen that little girl coming in and out of the house in the middle of the street every day.

Sometimes they heard her singing in the greenhouse.

Was she singing? Was that singing?

What noise? You might ask.

Oh, I don't remember, the neighbours would answer.

You see? The little girl was typical and yet, rather unusual.

But there was someone who knew her well. A little boy. He didn't go to her school. They played together in the park outside his house.

This little boy was not unusual at all. His friends, classmates, and teachers could tell you things about him at the drop of a hat. He said stupid things when he got flustered. He played the clown a lot but was much more intelligent than most people gave him credit for. He had the loudest laugh and was always the quickest to smile.

The two of them made an odd pair, running around in the woods, hurling leaves at each other, climbing trees, and playing the parts of pixies, elves, and ogres. The little boy could tell you almost anything about the girl. He could tell you the colour of her eyes, the things she liked, the things she hated. He could tell you the subjects she was good at and her favourite things to do. He could describe her smile to you. But if you asked him to, he probably wouldn't.

The little girl loved the little boy very much. When they were finished playing, the two of them would lie down in the grass. She would rest her head on his chest and listen to the way his heart pumped blood around his little boy body.

"I love you," she told him. "One day, when we're grown up, we should get married."

"I love you too," he told her. "We should. Definitely."

The little girl held that memory very close. She remembered the red-brown leaves on the trees. She remembered the rise and fall of his chest. She remembered how comforting it was to lie there like that. The grass had been a little damp. She could feel the mushy brown earth beneath her right hand. She wanted to stay that way forever. In that moment, everything was perfect. It was like the falling leaves stayed still.

The world froze, and there was only the two of them.

*

The little girl and boy grew up in no time at all. Perhaps not old enough to get married, but old enough that their worlds grew large and full. The boy's world seemed enormous. He had many friends and even a girl he really liked.

If you asked his friends, classmates, and teachers, they would tell you that the boy was a wonderful actor. He had played the lead role in three school productions. They would tell you he was still the quickest and loudest to laugh. They would tell you he was kind and liked to make those around him happy. They would tell you that he wanted to be a news reporter and was going to study journalism at university when he was old enough to go.

As for our girl, well, her classmates and teachers still couldn't tell you much. A couple was certain she had hobbies, perhaps an after-school club? Which one? Well, they had not really thought about it. They would tell you that she wasn't quiet in class, but none of them could recall the kinds of things she said, or describe the sound of her voice. She wasn't alone, but nobody was sure who her friends were.

There was the boy, of course—the boy from another school, whom she was sometimes seen hanging around with.

Though the boy and girl still spent a lot of time together, things were different. They would meet in the clearing in the woods, and she would help him learn the lines for his plays. He would make her laugh, but nowadays, he noticed the laughter didn't reach her eyes. He would tell her about the friends he made in his plays, the classmates he got on well with. He would suggest introducing her to his group, but she always politely refused. In fact, the more the boy thought about it, the more difficult it was to say he understood what she was thinking. Sometimes as they sat against the trees, he would wonder what she felt as she read him his lines. What did any of this make her feel? What must it be like to be so empty?

It made his skin crawl.

He didn't tell her when he got a girlfriend. How could he? He had no idea how she would react. They weren't children anymore. The girl was his friend, but he didn't know what she thought or felt about anything. He had forgotten the promise they'd made amongst the red and brown leaves when they were children. He had a mind only for his future as a journalist and his beautiful, sweet girlfriend. How happy and together his world was at the moment.

One day he brought his girlfriend to the clearing in the woods outside his house. It was autumn. The ground was covered with red and brown leaves. He kissed her softly, and they sat down on the crunchy damp ground. The boy was content. Everyone who knew him could see his smile was brighter than ever. His laugh was at its loudest.

He smiled at the girl when she stepped into the clearing. She smiled back at him, but it did not reach her eyes. He introduced her to his girlfriend.

His girlfriend liked the girl, though she could not tell you what colour the girl's eyes were, or what her smile had looked like. His girlfriend was not even sure how the girl had introduced herself. But she had liked her. His girlfriend had left the two of them in the clearing because the girl had told her that somebody at home was looking for her. His girlfriend did not particularly wonder how the girl would have known this. It sounded right.

The girl waited patiently for his girlfriend to leave the woods before she spoke.

"Why didn't you tell me?" the girl asked.

"I didn't know how," the boy answered.

"But you should have told me."

"I didn't know how you would react," he told her.

"What do you mean?" the girl asked. "Nobody in the world knows me like you do."

"I don't," the boy said. "I can never tell what you're thinking." He started to think it was strange his girlfriend had left because the girl had told her to. He was pretty sure she did not know any of his girlfriend's family.

"I love you," she told him. "Don't you remember that?"

The boy looked embarrassed. He remembered it now. It felt childish and silly for her to bring that up. It felt like an eternity ago.

"Come on, we were only kids."

"It doesn't matter. I love you."

The girl reached out and took his hand in both of hers. Her hands were cold and damp, her palms so rough.

"I love you. I love you. I love you. We are supposed to be together."

She said it like a mantra, like a spell. If she said it enough, he would agree with her. Just as his girlfriend agreed that a family member needed to speak to her.

"Why are you saying that? Do you even know what love is?" The boy asked, taking his hand away from hers. "Stop it. Love isn't about demands. You don't even understand that, do you? You're full of secrets, and it scares me, honestly!"

"It's not like that," the girl said. "You see all of me. That's how it's always been."

"I love someone else," the boy insisted.

"But I love you," the girl repeated. Her rough-palmed hands pressed against her own chest as if she were finding it hard to breathe. "What . . . what am I supposed to do with these feelings if you don't want them?"

The boy looked at his feet.

"I have to go."

You know, I remember exactly how that girl looked when she smiled.

*

Once upon a time, there was the most unusual couple. The woman was neither pretty nor ugly, thin nor fat. Amongst the women in her office, she never really stood out. She could be that woman stood beside you on a crowded rush-hour train. Or maybe that woman sat drinking a cup of coffee in a café. But this woman existed all the same.

The woman was not openly unusual, but if you were to ask a co-worker or her boss to describe her more closely, you would definitely find a pattern.

And her neighbours were sure they had seen that woman coming in and out of the house in the middle of the street every day. Sometimes they heard her singing in the garage. Was she singing? Was that noise singing?

What noise? You might ask.

Sorry, did I say something? Her neighbours would answer.

Perhaps you know where I'm going with this?

As for the man, well, he is something of a stay-at-home husband.

*

The room was cold and always so wet. The man had twenty-four windows to look out of. There wasn't much of a view, but he was content. It was safe here. He never had to work particularly hard. And, of course, he had the love of a good woman. What man could ask for more?

There was always something to eat. She hadn't been the best cook at first. In fact, as he recalled, when they began living together, her cooking was so bad it made him sick. The smell of the food had been so rancid he could not eat it. But now everything she made tasted delicious. What other man could say he had a woman to cook him yummy meals every day?

What other man could say he had a woman who loved him as much as she did.

He could hardly wait for her to get home from work. She

always brought him something good to eat. She would reach through the bars of his room and stroke his cheek with her rough-palmed hands.

The man would only have to look into her eyes, and a chorus of words would pour down on him, filling him up. He had everything he needed to know about the world in her eyes.

I love you. I love you.

"I love you, too."

An Interested Party

Initially, Roy started spying on his neighbours in the 1980s. At the time, they'd been a group of students, and he suspected them of being precisely what they appeared to be—a bunch of drugged up, over-sexed slackers who would never make it in the real world. The boys had permanent insolent smirks. The girl wore skirts too short and had no respect. She was in a relationship with one of the boys, though Roy could never tell which one.

Their manners, unfortunately, weren't the only source of irritation for Roy. They hosted parties every night. This was something he raised with his landlady, Mira, who dismissed it. Of course, it didn't matter to her; she didn't live in the building. Roy would finish a long day at the factory to come back to red-eyed students smoking in the corridor, chuckling at his overalls.

The girl and whichever of the boys she was dating would make love into the early hours of the morning in the room adjacent to Roy's. The sound of the girl's exaggerated screeches made his loneliness that much more so.

Ultimately, it was loneliness that compelled him to get rid of them.

Despite Mira's laxness as a landlady, she seemed to think that she ran a classy establishment catering to both students and young professionals. Because of this, she had two rules: no drugs, no pets.

Roy bought the listening device from one of the guys in the factory. They were always breaking things. That time, it was the washing machine. He piped up a conversation with one of the boys and offered to fix it. Though happy to accept his help, the young man, whose name Roy now no longer remembered, wasn't interested in him and so left him to his own devices and took a shower while Roy worked.

The device was placed in a weak spot in the wall, damaged by damp and entirely concealed. The wire, one that Roy had fashioned himself that connected to another in his apartment, fed through a hole at the back of the damp spot.

The suspicion of drugs was proved quickly. From just hearing them, Roy knew they kept pills in the cupboards, they smoked pot around the breakfast table, the girl injected, and the boys did not. He confirmed that the girl was not seeing one of the boys, but both. Roy heard them rutting together on the floor like animals with unnerving clarity. Although the girl did not know how tender her boyfriends were to each other when they were alone.

Of course, he couldn't show his findings to Mira. He did, however, keep on at her, insisting they did drugs, that he could smell something funny coming from theirs. She maintained that she had inspected the flat on multiple occasions, to which Roy scoffed and said she had given them time to prepare. Though she disliked him immensely, for once, Mira took his advice.

The surprise inspection of the apartment sent the three of them packing within a week.

The next people Mira let the place to were just as unsavoury. A grubby looking woman with sagging breasts and her child who spat on the floor and screamed at anyone who spoke to him. The device was there as a precaution. She beat that boy regularly, cursing over the television that blared through the walls of Roy's apartment like a foghorn.

"That child has cigarette burns on his arms," Roy said to Mira when he paid his rent.

Child protection was called, and the flat was empty again.

New people came over the years, but Roy was never able to justify stopping. In fact, as technology moved on, he found some reason to visit his neighbours so he could upgrade from listening to watching.

The current tenants were young professionals just out of university. Friends, from what he could tell. Both girls, they had the decency to pop round and introduce themselves when they first moved in three months before.

They made a curious pair of room-mates. Ravi was very tall for a woman. She was Asian with freckles scattered across her long, thin nose and high cheekbones. Her black hair was cut short and framed her face. She shook his hand like a man might have. Roy was initially impressed by her, though he disapproved of her shorts which exposed her long legs. Sawyer, the other girl, was small and slender with wide eyes, a heart-shaped face, and long blonde hair that came to her waist. She dressed conservatively, always in pastel blouses and wide legged plain trousers. She spoke softly, always at one gentle pitch. It was pleasant to his ears through the thin wall. Roy had, in fact, upgraded the camera (under the guise of repairing the toaster) to get a better look at Sawyer.

Ravi worked in the city, she told him, as an editor for a publishing house. She got to work with some eccentric authors. Her job kept her away, sometimes travelling to different parts of the country. Her absence left Sawyer alone often, not that she seemed to mind. Sawyer worked from home, designing costumes for a theatre company.

The camera was placed in the hallway, with a view of the kitchen and the spare bedroom Sawyer used for a studio. Having retired from his job at the factory, Roy was content with keeping up to date with his neighbours.

Sawyer was hard working. She would sit with her knees pulled to her chest, resting her sketch pad on her thighs, chewing her pencil as she thought of her next design. He liked to think of her like that as he went to sleep at night. The gentle curve of her calves, her focused blue eyes and the pencil that rested on her plump bottom lip.

Oh, to be that pencil.

Despite the beauty of her designs and her prowess with a sewing machine, Sawyer was actually rather clumsy when it came to hand stitching. Her work was often interrupted with cries of 'Owch! Shit!' when the needle caught her fingertips. She was cute like that—frantically waving her injured hand, calming down and blowing on the tips. Then she would sigh, put down the current garment and stomp over to the chest of drawers where she kept an unsurprisingly large supply of plasters.

When the hard part was done, the actors would come over to the apartment for their fittings. They were an odd assortment of people. Beautiful young men with muscled thighs and arms, who blushed as Sawyer stood up on tiptoe, gently pressed against them as she adjusted collars or refitted buttons. There were chubby middle aged men who joked with Sawyer to 'not tell the wife' about this. There were thin middle aged women who looked down their nose at her, whose bare, stretched skin showed the passage of time that they attempted to hide with makeup. And there were lovely young girls too, girls who laughed through the walls, who wore decorative underwear. Those girls kept him up at night.

The current arrangement next door would have suited Roy just fine the way it was, but then one day, after a particularly dull afternoon playing cards with his brother-in-law, Roy returned home and logged onto the computer to check the camera feed. Today Sawyer had mostly stuck to her studio, sketching. She went on the phone for half an hour, he didn't know who she was speaking to, but the call seemed to upset her considerably.

The crying shocked him. He felt helpless. Roy imagined sitting beside her, wrapping his arms around her thin torso and holding her while she wept. But of course, he couldn't.

She calmed down and made another call. One of the young men from the theatre company arrived. They sat together on the sofa in the studio for a little while, talking and laughing. Then they were kissing, holding each other, pulling at their clothes, and grinding their bodies together.

Roy watched, startled, as those conservative clothes came off. She was even lovelier that way—soft, supple, with perky breasts and nipples like pink rose petals. The young man, whose name she kept calling, 'Tom, Tom! Tom!' clung to her hips as she rode him astride the sofa. Her hand struck Roy's wall as she moved frantically, long blonde hair swaying.

The urge to touch himself had been gone for so long that his own passion surprised him. The quickness of his orgasm, the beating of his heart—it was a rush. He finished, panting, his hand dirty as he watched the two of them climax. Sawyer clung to Tom's neck as she sobbed out in bliss.

Their romance was passionate but infrequent. Tom would visit during those quieter, more intimate times whilst Ravi was away. It made sense; Sawyer was a real lady, prim and proper. Roy suspected that her passion was embarrassing to her. She didn't want her friend to know what she was like. He could tell that Tom was in love with her. Sometimes the two of them would have dinner first or watch a film. Roy would listen to their chatter—Sawyer's gentle laugh—before they moved to the studio to devour each other.

Roy watched them do it in every way, take on every position. He would make sure that he was home so he could watch them on the screen and hear them through the wall. Every time, he would come with them, clasping his wrinkled cock with the excitement of a teenager. He would press his face against the wall to better hear Sawyer's desperate little groans and moans as she approached climax. He would close his eyes and imagine being there. Her young, soft skin against his withered body. Tom's strong hands against his hips. His lips on Roy's throat, Sawyer's covering his own.

His own hands on himself began to feel like theirs. Yes, he

was with them when he closed his eyes.

For a little while, it was enough for him. Even his brother-in-law commented on his new, upbeat attitude. Roy would return to his apartment, no longer feeling like he was coming back to more of his own company. He found himself craving Ravi's business trips that sent her far away and Tom and Sawyer back into his bedroom.

"How do you do?" he chirped to Sawyer as they met at the post slot downstairs.

"Very well, thank you. And how are you, Roy?"

She was always so formal. He wanted to tell her that she didn't need to be with him.

"All good here," he said, grinning at her. "Do you have any plans for the day?"

"Just work, I've got fittings all afternoon," she said.

"With Tom?" he asked.

She didn't blush as he imagined she would.

"Oh, do you know Tom?"

"A little," he said. "He's a lovely young man."

"Yes, I suppose so. He's good to work with." She tucked her post into her handbag. "I hope you have a nice day, Roy."

It's just us, Sawyer, he wanted to say. It's just us.

Leaving yourself open made it easier to be hurt. He knew every inch of her, knew how she liked to be touched, where she liked to be kissed. And yet, she spoke to him as she would a near stranger. The current arrangement was not enough.

*

"Do you know the old man next door?" Sawyer asked.

"No?" Tom said, frowning. "Should I?"

"He said he knew you a little? Maybe he was confused."

He laughed and reached up for her. Sawyer's expression softened, and she pulled away.

"I think you should go."

"I really want to stay," he said.

"Tom, we've talked about this ..."

"I want to make this public. I really care about you."

"You know I can't," she said. "Tom, you know that."

He looked hurt as he pulled on his denim jacket and opened the studio door. "Fine."

The front door slammed, and Sawyer groaned in frustration, lying down on the bed and covering her face.

Roy switched off the monitor and went to his front door. Through the spy hole, he could see Tom leaning against the wall. His large brown eyes wet with tears. Initially, Roy was revolted. In his generation, a man wouldn't cry. But then his heart softened. Tom was different. Tom was an actor, sensitive, gentle. These were the qualities that Sawyer loved in him, despite her protests.

"Are you alright?" Roy asked as he opened the front door.

Tom was startled, colour flooding to those sculpted cheeks. "Sorry, I didn't realise I was being—"

"No, it's fine. There's no need to be embarrassed. Would you like to come inside?"

"No, no, I couldn't. I should be going."

Roy laid a hand on his arm. "Honestly, it's no trouble."

*

This was the next stage. Sawyer was a girl, shy of her own nature. She couldn't be his way in. Tom, on the other hand, was a friendly, extroverted leader. Roy planned to gain his trust, his friendship, console his wounded heart. He would help the two of them get together properly, live together in the flat next door. He would be their dear friend, the three of them laughing together around the dining table.

Maybe one day, Tom would slip his strong arms around him as Roy went to retrieve his coat. Sawyer would press her body against his and say in that soft voice, "Tom and I would like for you to stay the night."

Yes, that was how it would be.

"You're a good listener," Tom said. "I feel a little stupid blabbering on at you like this."

"Forget about it. When did it become crazy for two neighbours to talk to each other?" Roy said, chuckling as he topped up his drink.

"Oh, I don't live there," he said. "No, just kind of visiting, I guess."

"You two aren't dating?"

"It's complicated. I mean, I want that, but it's like there's a wall between us." Roy felt very much the same. "I don't know," Tom continued. "We're so close one second, and the next, she's looking at me like I'm a stranger." His eyes watered as he spoke.

He really was sweet. Roy's hand trembled under the table, longing to wipe away those tears.

"Have you told her how you feel?"

"Loads of times," he said, putting down his glass, a drop of whisky lingering on his lips. He drank too much; it was an unsavoury quality in so many of today's young people. But Roy could forgive him for that. He was Tom. His Tom.

"Sawyer is a very guarded girl. She's old fashioned that way," Roy said, nodding. "I think she keeps her public and private selves separate. Merging them would be unsettling for her. That's why she resists you. She'll come around. I can tell she's lonely when you're not there."

Tom's eyes narrowed. "I didn't realise you and Sawyer were close."

"We are neighbours, after all. Friends really. We are closer than you'd first think."

"Right," he said.

"She confides in me," Roy said. "I think she is quite fond of me. You know, if I were thirty years younger." He laughed. Tom didn't. "Well, I suppose age is just a number after all. As neighbours, anything could happen."

There was something strange about Tom's expression, something Roy couldn't read.

"Listen, I'm grateful for the talk and the drink. But I really should be going. I have a rehearsal to get to."

"A rehearsal?" Roy repeated. "Is it wise to go when you've been drinking?"

"You'd be surprised. It is the acting scene, after all," he said with an anxious chuckle.

Why are you so nervous? It's just me, Roy wanted to say.

Tom laced up his boots, more quickly than usual, like he was afraid of something. It was unfathomable.

"Tom," he said, "why the hurry?"

"No hurry, I just have to dash," he said. "The director is a real stickler for tardiness."

Roy reached down and touched his chin, making him look up at him. His stubble tickled the wrinkled crevices of Roy's fingertips. "Don't go," he said. "Please, stay with me a little longer."

"Listen, I think you have the wrong idea about me," Tom said.

"What's the matter with you? It's just me." Roy reached for him again.

Tom stood up, one of his boots still unlaced. He batted Roy's hand away. "Don't touch me."

"Tom," he said, trying to hold him.

Those strong arms shot up and shoved Roy hard.

"I said no! What are you doing?"

"I know what you like," Roy said. "Your ears are sensitive, so is the back of your thigh. But she won't suck your cock. I would, Tom. I'd do that for you."

The disgust on Tom's face was hurtful. This wasn't how it was supposed to be. This wasn't like Tom at all.

"You're sick," he sneered.

He would go and tell Sawyer, Roy realised. She would get upset. She'd move, and Roy would never get the chance to tell her how he felt. He would never get to lie beside her.

It seemed obvious then that Tom could never leave.

Roy hit him in the back of the head with his cane. His lovely face smacking into the front door, and he fell to his knees.

Stunned from the blow, Tom turned and looked up at him, confusion and fear in his eyes as he was cut.

There was no noise. In moments, he had gone from being the loveliest man Roy had ever seen to nothing more than a bloodied mess on the carpet. Roy removed his clothes with tenderness, caressing the uncut skin. How beautiful he was in person, still warm and sculpted. Roy knelt beside him, lovingly kissing his muscles, the curve of his elbow on the dangling right arm. He held Tom's head close and kissed him.

This was almost as good as the real thing.

He lay on the hallway floor, amongst the parts of Tom. For a time, Roy was content, and then he realised that he had done Sawyer a great wrong. He had stolen her lover away. The guilt consumed him as he thought of her lying alone on the bed in tears.

What had he done?

It was as he washed the blood from his hands that he found a solution.

*

Sawyer checked her phone again. He hadn't replied to her apology. Maybe it was for the best. She put the coffee cups back in the cupboard, lest Ravi wonder why she had used two, and walked back into her studio.

If Tom didn't want to see her again, she decided that she would pass his costume onto Gregor to finish. It would be too hard for them to go on as usual.

She was putting the half-finished costume back into the wardrobe when there was a knock at the door. Ravi had her key. She frowned and glanced at the peephole. The glass was smudged and dusty, but she could faintly make out Tom's face.

Opening the door, she said, "What is it? You know you can't be here tonight . . ." Her words died in her throat when she looked at him. Tom stared back at her. Well, it was Tom's face, horribly stretched over a longer face. The skin sagged around dark eyes framed with wrinkles. It looked like blood in his hair. The neck drooped. But he wore Tom's clothes, the clothes he had left in that afternoon. The stranger's feet squelched in his boots.

Sawyer bit back a sob as the stranger reached for her. Tom's hands that she knew so well stretched like gloves over small claw-like fingers.

The stranger wearing Tom's skin was breathing heavily. Glancing down, Sawyer could see Tom's jeans straining against his erection. She screamed when he touched her and tried to slam the door onto him. His shoulder crashed into it, and he lunged at her. His hand narrowly missed her hair as she ducked and ran.

Ravi kept a bat in the kitchen above the cupboard. Sawyer slammed the kitchen door closed and pushed the bin against it. Her heart was pounding in her ears, Sawyer's eyes prickled with tears as she reached around for the bat. Her hands clasped around it, and she held it in front of her protectively.

"HELP! HELP ME!" Sawyer yelled. "SOMEONE!"

"Sawyer, come out," the man called. He was doing an impersonation of Tom's voice. "It's only me. There's no need to be afraid."

He kicked the door hard, and the bin skidded.

"Get out of my flat! GET OUT!" she yelled, bashing the bat against the door.

"You shouldn't raise your voice. That's not like you."

"Please go! Please . . ." Tears trickled down her cheeks, her breath heavy. Her hands were slippery on the bat. "Why are you doing this?"

"I want to touch you," he purred. "I want to hold you. I know how you like it."

He peered at her through the gap.

"You pretend to be sweet and shy, but I know you're a little slut."

He was pushing against the door, grunting from the effort. Sawyer stepped back, trying to steady her hands. All she had to do was hit him once.

The stranger staggered through the door, palming himself over Tom's jeans. Sawyer let out a shout and lunged at him. The blow caught his shoulder and knocked him to his knees. He howled and grabbed onto the bat when she went to hit again. He was trying to pull it away from her. Sawyer kicked him as hard as she could between the legs. He grunted and dropped to the ground. Still clasping the bat, Sawyer had to let go as she scrambled over him, running now for the studio.

She could lock herself in there—use her computer to contact the police. He grabbed her from behind and pulled her against him. He smelled of blood, of rot, of stale food. She kicked and thrashed as he lifted her off her feet. He clung to her, the dead skin of Tom's face bulging when the man beneath tried to kiss her neck. Tom's hands touched her waist and legs as the man carried her to the bed in the studio.

Sawyer kicked him when he tried to pin her down. The man's hand shot out and struck her across the face. The hit was so hard that the skin of Tom's hand came off and slapped against the headboard. The flesh beneath was withered, wrinkled, and gnarled.

"You aren't that kind of girl, Sawyer," he said, no longer impersonating Tom. "It's not in your nature to act like this."

"Please don't hurt me . . ." she begged. "I don't know why you're doing this."

"Because I adore you," he said. "I wouldn't leave you alone." He ran his withered hand along one trembling leg. "I know all the things you like." He bent his head, and his tongue poked out through Tom's mouth to lick along her neck. He was harder than ever against her, his cock pressing into her stomach; every time she gasped or cried, he trembled with pleasure. "You're a dirty girl, and you want it all the time. I've watched you, I know."

She tried to roll onto her stomach when he started taking off her jeans, but he wouldn't let her. He held her down by her chest as he fiddled with her zipper.

"Sawyer," he cooed, "Lie down, lie still." He pulled the jeans off one pale leg. She was shaking, covering her face with her hands. "No need to play shy, it's only me." The withered hand slipped between her legs. "It's only me . . ."

He would rape her, wearing Tom's skin like a costume. Ravi would find her dead in the spare room like that. Ravi would come home and find her—

Sawyer opened her eyes as the abandoned bat smashed into the side of the stranger's head. Tom's face slammed into the wall. He grunted and slumped down on the bed beside her.

Ravi stood over the two of them, as Sawyer had feared so many times. It had been her worst nightmare before, Tom lying beside her in the bed, Ravi in the doorway, eyes wide and confused.

"Come on," she said frantically, "Babe, come on. Before he gets up!"

Her hand held hers and Sawyer rushed to her, clinging to her, weeping.

"Ravi, Ravi, I was so scared—"

"It's alright. Did he hurt you?"

Long fingered hands clasped her face, making her meet her gaze. Sawyer shook her head. Her legs were shaking.

"No. No, he didn't get the chance. B-But, he killed Tom."

"Tom? Who's Tom?"

"H-he . . . he was . . . he was one of the guys from the play."

"I'm calling the police. Come on," Ravi said, bending down to pick up her jeans. "Put these on. It's going to be okay. We can lock him in here and go wait somewhere else." Sawyer nodded, bundling her jeans against her chest.

Ravi handed her the bat, her hands shaking as she fiddled with her keys. "It's going to be okay. It's going to be okay." She repeated it a couple of times as she locked the door. "We can ask the old guy next door if we can stay at his until the police arrive. Sawyer, it's okay. Don't cry."

They stepped out into the hallway, Sawyer stumbling as she pulled on her jeans, propping the bat against the wall. She stepped in the trail of blood leading from next door to theirs.

*

The screen displayed a bloody bed, a glove-like hand on the pillows. An old man wearing the skin of a young man sat up on the bed. He groaned, his back ached. He glanced up at the camera through the holes in his borrowed skin. The lips of the young man's face stretched into a smile.

This was it. He was here.

NIGHTSHIFT

The front door of the restaurant—yes, company guide-lines are very clear about referring to this place as a *restaurant*—is locked when you arrive. You have to stand out there in the cold and the dark, knocking like a nosey neighbour, waiting for your manager to come and let you in.

She isn't pleased to see you and tells you before you're even through the door that some drunk girl has vomited over one of the tables, and you're going to need to clean it up. So with that to look forward to—and honestly, who wouldn't be looking forward to *that*—you enter the shop and begin what will be a very, very long nightshift.

10:00 PM

I don't know what it is, but there's something about cleaning up human waste that really puts your life into perspective. You'll never meet the drunk girl who left this mess here, but you find yourself hoping in your heart of hearts that she has a terrible night and is always a little bit ashamed of herself for vomiting in public. You have to scrub extra hard to get the chunky pink mess out of the grooves in the plastic seat where it has dripped from the table.

As you get up from bending over the chair, hands feeling stained even inside disposable plastic gloves, you glance up and see your manager, Hazel, and Karen, with the weird laugh, stood by the counter, surveying you with bored amusement.

Hazel has taken a real dislike to you as of late. Quite often, a shift with Hazel has you finding yourself imagining scenarios where she has plied some random drunk girl with milkshake and more vodka to make her vomit just so you have to clean it up. You scold yourself for being ridiculous and decide to placate your resentments by imagining pushing Hazel head-first into the fryer.

This makes you smile as you take off your gloves and douse the table and chair for a third time with anti-bacterial spray, rubbing it lovingly into the shiny plastic until the bubble-gum pink vomit is a thing of the past.

You're putting the cleaning products away when Hazel snaps at you to get to the kitchen and take over from Cathy on the headset. You barely have time to toss out your dirty, vomit-stained gloves and wash your hands before Hazel is beside you.

She brandishes the headset at you, forcing you to take it in your slippery wet hands and awkwardly place it onto your head. She has turned crimson, spittle on her lip as she bellows, "When I say NOW, I mean NOW!"

Karen and Phil are watching from the drinks counter, both smirking. Karen creases up in laughter and ducks out of sight. You notice that her face wrinkles when she laughs, giving you a sneak preview of Karen at age seventy. It fills you with a vague sense of satisfaction as you trudge over to the payment window.

"For God's sake, can you try coming to work awake for a change?" Hazel says, following you with her arms folded. "We're short-staffed tonight, so don't get on my nerves, okay? Think you can manage that."

And I mean, how are you even supposed to respond to that? So you say "sure" and trudge away. She loudly mimics your 'sure.' which gets a big laugh from Karen and Phil. Well, Hazel, aren't you the comedian?

11:00 PM

Sometimes when you're working on the headset, you begin to imagine that you're a robot. You think you could easily do this job if you were a robot. Would it even count as a job then? Or would this just be . . . your function?

Scratch that. It's more depressing for you to think of this place as your function.

You kind of like to think of your job as your benefactor. It funds who you get to be when you aren't in this stupid, starchy uniform with the itchy hat and clunky headset. Some people have super rich parents or a helpful dead grandma. You have a job in a fast-food restaurant.

Aren't you a lucky thing?

Now, if this were a day shift, then working the headset would be a best-case scenario. I mean, you get a little booth, away from Hazel and the others, just you, the headset, the window, and the till. Sure, the customers can be shitty, but it's the least amount of interaction with them you can get in a customer-facing job. They drive to the screen, you take their order, they drive to your window, and you accept their payment.

The worst thing that can happen is running out of change and needing to venture away to get more from Hazel, who, nine times out of ten, tells you to just *'manage'* it out of pure spite. But hey, it beats having her be a bitch to you whilst also frantically putting an order together or something like that.

Day shifts on the headset are where it's *at*.

However, you haven't had a day shift in months.

Nights are another kind of beast entirely.

Sure, there are the benefits of the booth, the safety from Hazel, the fact that it's just you, the headset, the window, and the till . . . but getting coherent orders and correct payments from night-time customers are a bit more complicated than their day-time counterparts. You become very aware of the line of cars beginning to pile up outside the store as you watch the red-faced bald man counting out change from the back of his taxi.

He tries to give you a button to compensate for one of the missing coins and calls you a 'goddamn fucking liar' when you tell him again, 'No, that's a button.'

"What the *fuck* are you doing?" Hazel hisses at you from the door to your booth. "Do you know how many cars are outside?"

You shrug at her before switching back to your headset, wincing miserably as a very drunk sounding car full of girls yells "WOOOOOOO!" down from the drive-thru window. That's another order paid in buttons, you think to yourself. On the headset, the group of girls start arguing with each other about what to order—one of them has a piercing laugh.

"... No, I said already. This is a button," you say to the drunk guy, holding it up for him.

In the background, you hear Hazel saying, "Sometimes I want to smack that gormless face of hers!"

You know how she feels; you feel the same way about her after all, but replace 'sometimes' with 'always', and you'd have a more accurate statement.

12:00 AM

The 'restaurant' is short-staffed recently, and nobody wants to work nights. Which means Karen got to go home already, leaving just you, Hazel, and Phil. You wouldn't usually mind this. Hazel is often less of a bitch when she has less of an audience.

"You know you have cleaning duty later," Hazel tells you as you retrieve a fresh stash of $1 bills from her. "This place is filthy."

"Sure," you say.

She rolls her eyes at you. "And I know we've had this little talk before, but nightshifts are busy. You need to be faster on the payment window. You got it?"

"Sure, Hazel, I got it."

"Are you sure about that?" she says, stepping in front of you to block your way back to the booth. "Because I'm not completely sure you do, College."

Oh yeah, her big thing at the moment is to call you 'College.' It's not really an insulting nickname, but she manages to make you feel like it is. If you ever make a mistake—and you know Hazel is always looking out for one—she's there, quick as a flash, saying something like, 'Wow, they'll really let anybody into college these days, won't they? College-girl here can't even count.' She likes to have an audience for stuff like that.

"I understand just fine," you say. "Call it my education paying off."

She doesn't like that. Her mouth turns back into a long thin line. "Just do your damn job, okay?" she snaps before storming off to talk to Phil. When you started this job, she was nice for a week and then went bad. You assumed it was some kind of company hazing, like managers getting in your face to see if you would cut it as an employee.

Nope, they don't seem to do that here. Phil started just two months ago, and he's been treated like one of the family.

"College! CAR!" Hazel yells.

Rolling your eyes, you head back to the window.

"Welcome to Mac's—" It feels so stupid to have to say 'Welcome' to customers like it's some honour to be here, like they're some cherished guest and not just here to spend $5.99 on quick, fast, shit food. "Can I take your order?" You hate that part of the greeting too. Like, what the heck else could you be doing? What, are they going to say no?

"Hey, is that Taylor? It sounds like Taylor."

Oh, God. You glance down at the little video screen of the drive-thru. You've come to know that particular car very well. This customer is a regular. His name is Frank, and he thinks of himself as a bit of an American Hero around here. The guy is a volunteer in the sheriff's department. He brags about seeing some action in the military, but you have sincere doubts he has actually served anywhere. However, Candice, the Branch Manager, has a real thing for fucking Frank, so he gets free fries with his meal. He calls them 'Hero's Fries,' which gives him all the credibility of a grown man in a Bat-suit consisted of hockey pads and a felt-tip mask.

He always comes here late. He *always* wants to chat to whoever he sees at the payment window. When he comes in to use the bathroom, some drunk always sees him do it and starts demanding the same treatment. His 'Hero Fries' are a nightmare to log on the till, and he really stares at your name badge (your tits), so he can say your name at the end of every sentence, in a way that makes you feel violated.

Fucking Frank rubbed you the wrong way from the very beginning. It was your first nightshift here, and he parked up his car and tried to follow you back into the restaurant. You explained to him that once the main shop was closed, customers aren't allowed inside. And he smiled this big, condescending grin and said, 'Oh, I'm not a regular customer, hon. Why don't you let me inside?'—the worst part was that Hazel really bit your head off about it.

'Oh, don't be too hard on her,' Fucking Frank had said, shit-eating grin on his face. 'She wasn't to know. Hey, you'll get used to me around here, hon.'

Ergh.

"Hey, sorry, the line isn't very clear," you say. "Welcome to Mac's. Can I take your order?"

And yes, it's petty, but it's your preferred method of dealing with him. No familiarity, this isn't some adorable family business, this is a fast-food joint. You aren't going to give him the Mom and Pop treatment he so desperately thinks he deserves.

So even though you know him so well that you spend hours thinking about him, hoping he gets shot while he's out pretending to be a real cop, you always begin every encounter like you've forgotten who he is.

"Taylor?" he calls, laughing. "Is that you?"

"Can I take your order?" you ask.

"Sure, sure, can I get a Scrumpy Burger with some of those hero's free fries?" he asks. You can imagine the stupid face he's probably making right now. Ergh, why didn't he die in whatever war he claimed to have fought in?

"Okay, do you want to order a drink with your meal?"

"Oh yeah, hon, I'd like a banana milkshake with that. One of the large ones."

"Right, that should come to $6 altogether. Please drive to the payment window."

"I know, hon, it ain't my first time."

You have two seconds of peace before Hazel appears at the door to your booth.

"College, do you not know MATH? You've undercharged the customer on the fries. It should be $7.50, College, come on!"

"It's Frank," you say, and there's a struggle not to say 'Fucking Frank.'

"What? I just said that—" She trails off as Fucking Frank in his fucking car appears. He beams at you, leaning out of his window. "Oh, hey, Frank, how's it going?" she says, all charm and sweetness.

"Well, hey there, Hazel, baby," he says, beaming at her. "You girls having a quiet one?"

"Oh yeah," Hazel says. "If College over here can manage to stay awake." She elbows you a little too hard in the side. "College, why don't you start getting Frank's order together."

1:00 AM

It's not even halfway through the night, and you're exhausted! She really does have it in for you this shift. You're spending it dodging between your payment window, the headset, and cleaning the shiny metal kitchen cabinets. It's not too busy tonight, but consistent enough that you aren't getting that far with the cleaning, and you're out of breath every time you rush to take an order. The cleaning product they insist you use here stinks, and you know your hands are going to carry that smell for a long time after you manage to quit this gig.

Hazel is holding court, a truly impressive thing, with only Phil to watch her. She's in the middle of some big long story about the *crazy* thing that happened when she went for her weekly shop. She only stops to bellow 'THERE'S A CAR THERE, COME ON!' at you whenever a customer starts heading through the drive-thru. She seems to enjoy doing this the most when you're bent over at an awkward angle, on your hands and knees scrubbing.

"CAR! NOW!"

You scrabble to your feet and rush over to the payment window. You hear the others cackling with laughter, and your face grows hot despite yourself.

"Welcome to Mac's. Can I take your order?"

You hear hysterical laughter on the other end and then the screech of tyres. Hazel starts yelling at you that the order hasn't come up on her screen. The car speeds past your window—the driver leans out and spits over the closed glass before speeding off, tyres blazing into the night.

"What was that?" Hazel asks.

"A prank," you say. "He just spat all over the window and drove away. He didn't order anything."

She steps in closer and examines the mess over the window. She wrinkles her nose in disgust. "Ew. So, erm, yeah, you know you're cleaning that off, right? I don't want any other customers to see it."

"Sure, I can clean it from in here if I reach around—"

"No," she says. "You'll need to go outside to do a good job."

"You're kidding me," you say. "It's raining."

She smirks nastily at you. "Come on, College. I bet this will be easy for you." She doesn't even wait until she's out of earshot before she starts laughing.

And yeah, you could be upset. Alternatively, you could imagine a reality where Hazel trips and falls and lands face-first onto the burger station.

You can almost smell that sizzle.

*

That's two different bodily fluids you've had to clean up tonight. You're absolutely certain there was nothing about cleaning up bodily fluids in your contract. It's cold outside, and the spit has already partially frozen. It's tough to clean. That's really disgusting.

You've had guys throw drinks before—one very disgruntled customer toss his order back through the window, pelting you with chicken nuggets. It's always gross. But spit seems too far. What if you'd had the window open?

You hear a rustling in the bushes across the car park. Probably a rat running around, trying to keep out of the rain. You wince in disgust.

Spit satisfactorily cleaned up, you head back towards the restaurant entrance. Only the door is locked. You roll your eyes and knock on the glass. Squinting, you can see Hazel and Phil purposefully ignoring you from the counter.

You knock again.

"Hazel," you call.

The two of them glance your way, then start laughing. Hazel grasps hold of the counter-top to support herself, she's laughing that hard. You roll your eyes and knock again. It's raining pretty heavily now, and you're getting soaked. Then, you hear the rustling in the bushes again. Only this time, you hear very clearly, footsteps, like someone running around behind the restaurant on the other side of the car park.

You haven't seen a car. The restaurant is off the beaten track; it's not easy to get to without a car. Nobody walks here. Is it some drunk who jumped out of their taxi? You'd rather not wait around and find out.

You continue to knock on the glass.

Then your headset crackles to life. Someone is stood in the drive-thru. There's definitely been no car. It's been quiet for the last hour or so. What's going on?

Then you hear a voice, two people are talking to each

other. It's all mumbled at first, but then you hear, "Round the front . . . little . . . blonde."

You freeze.

Someone on the other end of the receiver snorts with laughter. It's a high, uncomfortable sound. It sounds . . . crazed, not drunk. It sounds alert. Wrong. It sends shivers down your spine, and no longer caring how it looks, no longer caring what Hazel and Phil will say, you start pounding on the door now with both hands.

There's someone out there. Someone hiding in the bushes. Someone watching you. Oh my God! You don't get paid enough for this! You really don't! Why did you agree to do a nightshift? Weirdos come out at night! You're going to fucking die because fucking Hazel has a complex about you going to college.

You can hear footsteps now, quick steps, someone is running around from the drive-thru window.

Your heart is pounding in your mouth as Hazel appears at the door, rolling her eyes, lips twisted into a sneer.

"Calm down," she says. "What—!"

You push past her and rush inside. You see him in a flash. He's running right towards the door. The fucking doors are closing too slowly. He's going to get in, he's going to—! But then they close together as he reaches them. He bashes his fist against the glass and spits all over them. You and Hazel are frozen to the spot.

He's tall, so tall his forehead nearly touches the top of the door. He's bald with a matted looking beard. He's wearing faded grey jeans and a dirty looking raincoat. But it's his eyes you notice, his eyes that you can't look away from. They are wide, practically bulging out of his head. His nose looks broken at the top. His mouth is twisted into a broad, horrible smile. Are his teeth white and sharp, or is your mind playing tricks on you? He presses up against the glass and licks it once before bashing his fist against the door again.

"Let me in," he snarls.

You stagger back. You can hear your teeth chattering

together. Hazel is stood still, one hand over her mouth in terror.

"What's going on?" Phil calls. He slides over the counter and freezes when he sees the man and starts swearing under his breath. "Hazel, Hazel, I think we should call the cops. Is the door locked? Is it?"

"Yes," you manage to say very quietly. "We should come away from the door." You start moving back towards Phil, but you're too scared to take your eyes off the guy. "Hazel, come on."

She turns and rushes past you; her hands are shaking. She's gone completely pale.

"Come back, baby!" the guy calls after her. "Come back over here and let me in."

Phil has run into the kitchen to check the back door. He yells that it's locked before returning, hands shaking with his phone. "We should call 911. Hazel, are you okay?"

She shakes her head. "No. No. Fuck, fuck—! Let's call the cops. Phil, you do it."

Phil starts shakily pounding on his phone and mumbling 'fuck' to himself with increasing intensity.

Hazel roars and rips the phone from his hands. "What's the matter with you."

"It can't find a signal."

The man is still there, he's just staring at the three of you. His bulging eyes following. He licks along the door again. One hand reaches down to the front of his pants, and he gives a customary squeeze. He looks crazy. How did he get here? What's he going to do?

"College," Hazel snaps at you. "Check the payment window. Come on!"

So encouraging that in times like this, she can still be a bitch. You rush past her and walk on over to the booth. Your booth. Your safe space away from everyone. You reach for the window latch when something smashes into it hard. The glass cracks but doesn't break. Through the cracks, you can see someone out there.

It's not the same man. There's someone else. Someone

stood out in the drive-thru where a car would usually be. He's wearing something over his head, like a pillow-case. You can't see properly due to the shattered glass. He's wearing a long black coat, his arms stretched out to either side of him.

"We've called the cops. You should leave!" you lie to him, trying to sound braver than you feel. He doesn't need to know that you're close to pissing your pants, does he?

He doesn't exactly respond, but he starts . . . chuckling. It sounds like he's speaking through a microphone. It echoes wrong in your ear. Then he tilts his head to the side and bashes his fist against the glass again.

And hey, you're only human, so you scream and fall back against the wall.

"SHUT UP!" Hazel is yelling at you from the kitchen. "Goddammit, College! Shut up!"

There's this weird . . . grunting noise. Like an animal, like a low-moaning animal. You stagger out of the booth and see that bald guy by the front door is still there. He's making that sound, that horrible, groaning sound. He isn't hitting the glass anymore, he's just stood there, staring at you all and making that sound, that horrible sound.

Then comes a banging noise. A loud sound, like someone running into a wall. You follow Phil through the stock-room to the back door. Something bashes hard into the door again, and the two of you flinch. In the background, you can hear Hazel frantically talking to herself. The guy out front is making more awful noises, like a cat now, high screeching meowing. Someone runs into the door again, causing Phil to leap back.

Phil yells. "You better FUCK OFF!"

You cover your mouth with your hands.

Phil leans up and peers through the small glass window above the door. He lets out a gasp and nearly falls to the floor. You go to look, but he grabs your arm, holding you back. You look and see him just shaking his head.

"Phil, let go."

You manage to break free and jump as someone bashes into

the door again.

"They won't be able to get in," you say. "This is solid. It's password entry only." You think if you say it out loud, you'll start to believe it. You peer up through the glass and see a woman with black hair that's sticking to her from the rain. She's wearing a long dark raincoat that looks muddy. She bashes hard into the door and stumbles back, limp, almost like a zombie, before trying again. She looks up and meets your gaze. Her eyes are like the man's, wild and crazed and bulging from her head.

She sees you looking, and her face twists into a blissful smile that makes the hairs on the back of your neck stand up. Then her shoulders start trembling as she begins to laugh. You can hear her through the door, a high-pitched, deranged sort of noise. Then she raises a hand, and you see a butcher knife. It looks like it could cut you through the glass. She waves it at you almost cheerfully, like a child with a toy.

You stagger back and nearly fall into Phil, who looks as though he could burst into tears.

"Come on," Hazel is hissing. "We're going to go and lock ourselves in the office. College, come on!" She grabs your arm and pulls the two of you along. "I've got the keys. We're just going to wait it out in there."

You reach the small, cramped manager's office. You have vague memories of coming in here for your interview, how the chair legs screeched when you pulled one out to sit. That should have been a warning against this place. This fucking place. As if the job wasn't unpleasant enough.

Hazel closes the office door and locks it before quickly taking the chair by the computer and wedging it up against the door handle for extra protection. You take a seat on the floor by the large cupboard. Phil just stands there, like a stunned, greasy statue. His hands raised up, clasping at the sides of his face.

"Why was she laughing like that?" Phil whispers. "Hey, College, why was she laughing?"

"How am I supposed to know?" you say.

2:00 AM

The three of you are sitting there in the dark. This office is small for one person. With the chair pressed against the door, all of you are seated on the ground. Hazel can't sit still. Every now and then, she moves to climb up onto the desk, or she'll stand. Phil hasn't looked up from the ground once and keeps muttering "Oh my God" under his breath.

"Phil, are you doing okay?" Hazel nudges him when he doesn't answer. Phil just shakes his head and hides his face in his hands. She groans and starts tapping her fingers along the desk.

"Has this ever happened before?" you ask because genuinely, you are curious.

"No!" Hazel snaps. "Do you think I would ever do a nightshift again if this were a common occurrence?" She rubs her eyes. "I . . . know this sort of thing can happen. But not in real life, you know?

"What if they're inside the store already?" Phil groans. "There's loads of places they could hide. What if they already got in?"

Hazel went quiet. She got up and moved carefully over to the office door. "Shut up, let me hear," she says, though neither of you were talking. She presses her ear up against the door. You find yourself leaning in, despite it all. And faintly, you can hear that horrible fake meow. It sounds like it's coming from the same place, but honestly, this room is so dark and so cramped, it's hard to tell what direction anything is coming from anymore. But it does sound like he's still outside.

"Can't we call the cops using the office phone?" you ask.

"No, we can't, College, because it doesn't work," she snaps at you. "It stopped working a little while ago, and Candice wouldn't pay up to have it repaired. Do you have any other fucking helpful suggestions?"

"One of us should go and try and get the other cell phones. Maybe one of them will get a signal," you say. You say 'one of

us' because you don't want it to be you, and hey, she does keep
reminding you that she's in charge.

"No," she says. "We're going to stay in here."

"Hazel, can we put the lights on?" Phil says. "Sitting in the
dark is freaking me out more."

"No, we can't," she says coldly. "Because if they get inside,
they'll be able to see where we are."

"Well, if they do get in, it won't take them long to guess we're
in here," you say because honestly, it's creeping you out as well.

"No, I'm in charge, so the lights are staying off," Hazel hisses.
"Fucks sake! Do you both want to be dead?" She looks spooky
in the dark. She's taken off her hat—against store policy—and
hairnet. Her long dark hair gives her the look of a horror movie
monster in the dim light of the monitor screen. "I'm in charge,
okay? Got that, College? What the fuck is wrong with you?"
She sniffles and covers her head with her hands. "Goddammit.
Goddammit."

Her muttering is interrupted by the sound of a car outside.
Your headset crackles to life. A customer! There's a customer
outside. Hazel is staring at you, and you think for a second,
she's about to demand you recite the fucking stupid greeting.

"Errrr, hello?" A voice slurs from the other end of the line.
"So, can I get like . . . twelve nuggets and some fries, please?"

"Hello!" you gasp. "Hello, you need to help us! There are
crazy people outside. Please, can you call the cops? We don't
have a phone in here and—!"

"Huh?" the guy says. "What're you talking about? I just
want some . . . fucking chicken nuggets, okay?"

"Look," you say, trying to stop yourself from yelling. "We
can't take an order right now. People are trying to get into the
store. Please, you have to call the cops! You have to!"

"Hey, look, unlike you," the guy slurs. "I've done a proper
day's work, I'm a fucking . . . attorney, sweetheart. So just do
your job and get me . . . twelve fucking, chicken nuggets, a large
fries and . . . Baby, do you want a Coke?"

"Yeah, sounds good."

"HEY!" Hazel snatches the headset right off the top of your head, nearly yanking your hair out as she does. "YOU NEED TO CALL THE COPS NOW! NOW! GODDAMMIT! THERE ARE PEOPLE TRYING TO GET INTO THE STORE! YOU NEED TO—!"

"Fucking bitch, I'm going to Burger King," the guy says. And we can hear the screech of his tyres as the two of them drive away. Hazel is holding the headset, her eyes wide and bloodshot. Her hands are shaking, and she mutters, "No, no, no," over and over again.

The headset makes a sudden screeching sound. There's someone on the other end of the line. There's a faint thump, like someone tapping the surface of the receiver.

"Hello in there," a voice whispers softly.

It's the woman from outside. She's shrill, her tone wavering as though she's drunk or high.

"Hellllloooooo in there. Can you let me and my friends inside now? I'd hate for things to get messy. Please, let us in, and we'll only hurt you a little."

Hazel lets out a frustrated gasp and switches the headset off completely. She thrusts it back into your arms.

"Fucking hell, College! That was our last chance!"

3:00 AM

Your legs hurt from cramp. You tried to stand up half an hour ago, but Hazel snapped at you for getting in the way. She is more tense than ever.

"Why didn't you grab more than one phone?" she growls at Phil.

Phil isn't up to answering anymore. He keeps shaking his head. This means that Hazel directs all of her anger at you. It seems so unfair that you and Hazel will be associated with each other forever if you do die tonight. Even being in this very frightening, very real situation, she can't stop herself from being a bitch. Surely the danger should put things into perspective, but no, she's going to die, still being all bitter and angry about your fucking education.

"Fucking hell, can't believe I'm stuck here with you," she says. "Oh my God . . ."

"Why don't you call your friend Frank?" you say because you can't help yourself. And why would you? She's made your job here utterly miserable. She's even making this situation miserable. She nearly left you to die out there with a crazy man. You find yourself wishing, just a little, that you'd pushed her out the doors before they closed.

Maybe they'd leave if they got at least one of you?

"Fuck you!" Hazel snaps. "Fuck you!"

"Fuck you!" you snarl at her. "I'm putting a light on!"

"I want a light on," Phil tries.

"Nobody is putting a light on!" Hazel yells. She moves to block your path to the light switch. "Sit down! You aren't advertising that we're in this room!"

"You're advertising it by yelling!" you hiss. "Keep your voice down! They clearly didn't teach you that in the school of fucking hard knocks!"

She shoves you hard, sending you back into one of the cabinets. "If they get in here, they'll search the cash register, find no money there, get bored, and leave." She says it slowly, spittle hitting your cheek as she speaks. "You understand?" Then her eyes widen slightly. "College, where is the money from your cash register?"

"What?"

"Did you bring the money from your till?"

"Of course not, they started smashing windows, and we came in here!"

"College!" she cries out, exasperated now. "College! Are you serious?"

"I didn't," you say.

That feeling of dread is already pooling inside you because you know what's coming next. You can see that look on her face, even in the dark. The slight smirk, the twist of her lower lip.

That sadistic look in her eye, just like earlier, when she saw the spit all over the drive-thru window.

"Well, you realise you'll need to go and get it, right?"

"No!"

She grabs hold of your arm and squeezes tight. If you had better lighting, you know her face would be red. "You fucking get out there, College. Get your till! You get it right now! It's the only cash in the store!"

"There's money in the cash safe in here," you protest. "Honestly, there's nothing worth stealing in my till!"

"College, use your fucking head. If it goes missing, senior management could think we stole it."

"You're out of your goddamn mind," you snap at her. "I'm not going out there! This job isn't worth my life!"

"I'm not doing it," Hazel hisses at you. "You get out there, or when this is over, I won't just be firing you, I'll tell them that whoever robbed the store were friends of yours! I'll tell the cops that I heard you whispering outside with them. I'll tell them that!"

"That's bullshit!"

"You took an awfully long time out there, just to scrub some dirt off the window," she says. "Didn't she, Phil? I don't even know why you insisted on going outside to clean a window. I mean, we don't ask staff to do that. You went outside for a good amount of time!"

"You wouldn't let me back in!"

"And when you came back, suddenly there are three nutcases outside, trying to break in. And you conveniently leave your till out there for anyone to get!"

"Hazel, that's not true."

She hands you her keys. "Get out there now and fetch your till. While you're at it, grab your cell phone, College." She folds her arms, smiling—this fucking bitch is *actually* smiling. "Think you can manage that?"

And you'd say sure or anything else, but honestly, you have no words. You knew that fucking bitch wanted you dead.

4:00 AM

You waited as long as you could. Any longer, and she wouldn't have let you leave with the keys.

You slip out into the store, glancing nervously to either side of you. It's weird to have the lights on again. It's so bright that it takes a second for your eyes to adjust. To your left is the staff room; the door is closed, though the light is flickering eerily inside. The kitchen is on your right and completely empty. There's the faint smell of burning from a burger Phil must have left on the grill a few hours ago. You should get down low anyway, just in case the three of them are waiting by the front door, peering in.

I'm going to die doing this fucking terrible job, you find yourself thinking as you crawl along the floor back to your safe little booth and the till. Hazel has shown you which key you need to manually unlock the till. You just need to grab it and run back to the office. There's no point in trying to get into the staff room and fish through your bag for your phone too. You can just lie and say you thought you saw them about to smash a window and didn't want to give away your position. Yeah, something like that.

You glance up and see the glass is still cracked but not completely broken. You wonder why they haven't tried smashing it again. Maybe they're afraid of the alarms going off? You reach up with shaking hands and try to insert the key into the lock.

It won't go in. You get onto your knees in an attempt to examine it more closely. This is the wrong fucking key. She probably did that on purpose. The complete evil bitch! You half wish you were brave enough to just walk out through the front door and say to the creepy lady with the hair, 'Hey, I'm going. The others are hiding in the manager's office. Help yourself to the money in the till'. It's a tempting thought.

You start fiddling with the other keys. Why are there so many? What could some of these even possibly be for? You try to keep calm. You can hear that horrible meowing outside again. It sounds like the bald guy is walking around the perimeter of the restaurant, making that same noise. It's awful, and it makes it even harder to concentrate. You duck whenever he comes past the window. He peers right in, and you really do feel like you could piss yourself from pure terror.

Fucking Hazel would just love that.

The key clicks into the keyhole, and you let out a sigh of deep relief. You twist it in the lock, and it comes open with a satisfying clunk. Your hands are drenched in sweat as you manoeuvre the money tray out of the till. Your heart is hammering in your chest.

That's when the lights go out.

The bright lights of the restaurant make a funny sort of click, and then they're out. You're on your hands and knees, in the dark, holding your cash register, just frozen to the spot. Then you remember that the front doors are electric and likely on the same circuit as the lights. It's your last coherent thought before you hear the familiar snick of the front doors opening.

The meowing gets louder and louder.

In the darkness of the restaurant, you hear footsteps. You hear hushed whispering. You hear that horrible, high pitched laugh. Then you hear the scraping of a knife along the front counter. Why aren't you getting up? Why aren't you running?

You're on your feet, the till forgotten. It clatters to the floor behind you, spilling out coins all over. You're running back to the office, your heart pounding in your head. You hear someone rushing behind you, you hear hysterical cheering. Your hands fiddle frantically with the keys, and you manage to get the door open.

You see Hazel's face in the dark. She opens her mouth and seriously says, "Where's the till?" before there's a knife to your back. You feel Hazel reach out and snatch the keys from you, slamming the door shut in your face. Then there are hands over your eyes, and your world goes completely dark.

Previously

I know, I know, you kind of like to think of your job as your benefactor. It funds who you get to be when you aren't in this stupid, starchy uniform with the itchy hat and clunky headset. Some people have super rich parents or a helpful dead grandma.

You have a job in a fast-food restaurant.

Which, let's be honest, isn't much of a benefactor. I mean, you work so hard at this job, doing all these nightshifts so you can afford to pay for your classes, and you're failing your classes because you're so tired. Does that sound very fair to you?

And that manager of yours, God, she sounds awful! She calls you College, like you working for your education is something you should be ashamed of. What the fuck is up with that? You finish those shifts feeling more like an animal than a human being. You know the stupid menu backwards. You put in the time, and your co-workers treat you like shit. Is it worth it? You smell like an unsettling combination of industrial cleaning products and a deep fat fryer.

Again, is it worth it?

So, how about this, you can be your own benefactor.

Don't worry, I'll handle everything. You've moaned to me about your job enough for me to get a picture of what we'll need to do and when. Don't look at me like that. This will be fine. I've got a good feeling about this.

5:00 AM

This is the third bodily fluid you've had to clean this shift, you think, as you wash your hands in the sink. The cut on your back will hurt for a while, but hey, how will it look to the cops if we chopped up Hazel and poor Phil and you got away without a scratch?

You feel bad, but maybe you just think that because it sounds like something you should think. I mean, yes, two people are dead but come on, they sent you out there for the $200 in your cash register when they believed there were crazy people outside the store trying to get in. What kind of sociopath would do that?

Margie and Tony are loading the last of the cash into the back of their car. Andy is resting his vocal cords—you'll have to ask him how he got so good at making that creepy cat noise. It was ... unsettling and will probably haunt your dreams a lot longer than the deaths of Hazel and Phil will.

Didn't I tell you that you had absolutely nothing to worry about? We'll sort out the money when you get home from the hospital. You'll be fine giving your statement to the police. And when this all dies down, just think, you have the perfect excuse to quit this shitty job. Who on earth would want to stay and work somewhere where they got attacked with a knife and forced to hide in the dark all through the night?

This won't be as hard as you think.

So, you go and get your phone. You get yourself nice and worked up so you can call the police and really sell it to them. You can cry a little bit. Then, what you'll need to do is go and wrap yourself up in the freezer. You tell them that we dumped you in there. Keep it together just a little longer. Soon, you'll be home, and we can let the good times roll.

Of course we will. I mean, it's a big deal. You just worked your last nightshift.

SUCH STRONG HANDS

The first time you touched me, it was by accident. You were my brother Archie's handsome friend from Cambridge, roped into collecting me from that party. My brother passed out in the back seat. I sat up front beside you, too tipsy to remember to be shy. You were quiet, scowling the whole time. We drove back in near silence apart from Archie's snores.

A taxi swerved out in front of you on a roundabout halfway back to my parents' house. Your hand flailed forwards in the dark, searching for the gear stick. Instead, you found my knee and squeezed—your foot on the brake, the car screeching to a halt and stalling. Your face as you realised in horror that you'd grabbed me, the seventeen-year-old girl instead—you recoiled as if my bony leg had burnt you.

"Sorry!" you barked, actually barked at me. Red-faced, ears tipped crimson.

And I smiled and laughed and told you that it was fine, that I didn't mind, no really, I didn't! But you stayed like that, frowning and red-eared all the way home.

*

The second time we touched it was I who made the first move. A party for my father's birthday six months later. You had tagged along with Archie again. My brother flirted amongst the village girls he had left behind. But you stood at the back of the room, scowling with your arms folded. I wondered why you had even wanted to come.

The girl who lived across the road from me asked you to dance, and you barked—again, you barked—that you didn't dance, and she walked away, stunned and silent. Your bluntness often affected people like that.

A champagne and a half later, I strode over to you and grabbed your big hand in mine and tugged you out of your gloomy corner.

"Dance with me."

You dragged your feet and blushed and protested. But then you put your arms around me, and we danced. And you were dreadful, I'm sure you remember. You trod on my foot, and your ears ignited, but I laughed, and soon you were laughing with me. An abrupt sound, like distant thunder.

A warm sound.

*

The third time followed the day after. A stolen moment after breakfast before you and Archie drove back to university.

We met at the stairs. I smiled as you passed me, and you dropped the bulky backpack you were carrying on your foot.

Laughing, I bent down to help you, and you grabbed my small hand in your big strong one, and you kissed me right there on the landing. The bristles of your beard scratched my chin. Your mouth tasted of ash and blackberry jam.

Then you released my hand, picked up your bag and left me there, stunned.

*

After that, there was a fourth time, a fifth too, and after that, many, many times. Frantic kisses at the train station. Your big hands holding mine, encasing them whole. Your arms around me. Your warm palm on the small of my back, leading me upstairs. Your cramped student bedroom, your creaking bed, the itchy mattress, the spring that came loose of the linen and left a sharp indent on my knee. Bruises on my hips. Your mouth on my neck. My tongue in your ear. My nails raking rivers down your back. On your bed, over your desk, burns on my knees from the well-worn rug. Once, hurried in an alleyway, up against a wall. Your big strong hand over my mouth, crushing the sound out of me.

Trains back to my family home, the safety of my parents, the idle chatter of my friends. They all seemed like . . . children to me then. And on those long rides home, my whole body ached, sore from you, your touch seared into my skin. I ached, I ached for your hands on me again.

*

Of course my parents consented when you asked Father for my hand. My mother cried. Father called you 'son,' and we took a photo smiling and brilliant out in the garden.

And as you chatted with my parents, talking dates, and venues, I wandered away and found my brother smoking over the garden wall.

"Aren't you happy for me?" I asked.

He offered me the rest of his cigarette before lighting another for himself. "Be careful of that one, little sister. He's a good man, but he's out for himself. Keep your head screwed on tight."

And I laughed because you had always been Archie's good friend, and his warning seemed at least hypocritical. I mean, he was the one who laid me out before you. He was the one who put you in my sights.

*

Your parents adored me. I thought they seemed like us. Your father, so stern and abrupt. Your mother, with her wry smiles and way of winding a conversation wherever she wanted. I wanted us to be like them.

I loved your family.

Except your older sister. *Penelope.* I've come to dislike the name immensely. Even the way she writes it seems obnoxious. Christmas cards signed off with that flashy scrawl. Your brilliant older sister, who scoffed at doing chores, at anything written by a woman. She liked to think of herself as one of the boys with her tailored women's suits, love of strong spirits, and stylish short hair.

When I spoke, she would smirk as though I were telling a joke I wasn't aware of.

"You can't marry her," she said to you, while the two of you sipped brandy one night after your parents retired for the evening. "She's just a little girl."

And you threw back your head and laughed and wrapped an arm around me.

"Oh, Penny, really!"

You chuckled into your drink while I tried not to be irritated, tried to work out what response I could even give to a remark like that. Of course, there wasn't one, other than uncomfortably shifting into your arm, praying for a change of subject. And she knew it because she looked right at me and smirked.

Nasty creature.

But of course, the two of you have always gotten on like a house on fire.

*

You told me that you would make my dreams come true. And you have such strong hands that I believed you. I used to think there was nothing you couldn't do. So strong that I imagined you could carry me and you and our dreams all at once.

And despite it all, the day we married is still the best day of my life. My father walked me down the aisle to you. You took my hand in yours, and I left my childhood behind and moved into your world with you.

I had imagined that our life together, away from creaking beds and springy mattresses, would be a better, improved version of what we already had. You would work and come home to me, and we would lose ourselves in each other over and over and over again. I was finishing my degree, you were establishing yourself in your practice.

We came back from the Maldives, and I lost you to your job almost instantly. I'd return from classes, make dinner and wait for you. You'd return, weary and smug, sometimes you'd eat with me, sometimes you'd disappear into your office. I put up with it for a time. But as I ate alone more often than not, I decided I had to change things.

Do you remember the night I followed you into your study? I wore that red dress you liked. I slid your paperwork aside and climbed into your lap. I wanted you. I ached to feel your hands on me again.

And I did.

You closed one big, strong hand around my forearm and wrenched me bodily from your lap and out into the hallway like a misbehaving dog. My feet scrambled and stumbled against the carpet, struggling for balance.

You released me, and I felt your touch searing my skin.

Then you slammed the door in my face and left me there, stunned and silent.

*

You bought me flowers after. Red roses delivered that morning, two hours after you left for work. I took them from the pimple-faced teenage boy who delivered them and put them in water, in the vase your aunt bought us as a wedding gift. I put them on the table as a centrepiece. I imagined you sitting there at your office, feeling smug that you had resolved the ugliness between us. I imagined you coming home to me, sitting down for dinner, and as I poured your drink, I would take the vase and smash it against your skull, roses and all.

Bastard.

I trembled with rage all day. That night you managed to somehow sit at the table without your laptop, without your office. You pretended not to notice that I hadn't prepared your dinner. You followed me into the kitchen and took my hands in yours. You told me you loved me, that you adored me, that the thought of any harm coming to me filled your heart with dread. You kissed me again and again and again until I kissed you back.

Then you put me over the table, and I watched as the vase fell to the floor, roses and all.

*

We found ourselves in a time loop. You ignore me. You neglect me. I act up. You lash out. You apologise. We fuck. We fuck. We fuck. We fuck. Then you ignore me again. You don't see me, you make it all up to me and then switch on your laptop as I lie there beside you, spent. I rest my head on your shoulder, and it's like you don't even feel it, you can't even feel my hands on you.

You ignore me.

I lash out.

You have such strong hands, you leave bruises on my skin, purple bracelets, a necklace. Then you switch on your laptop, and I've lost you again.

So I *made* you see me.

I left our house, placed my wedding ring on the counter and went out into the night.

I went to so many bars. My course mates laughed and reminded me again and again that I never come out, how they couldn't believe I was there and we drank and drank.

You called me.

And I ignored it.

So many nights after dusty seminars and long lectures, they would go out and drink and live, and I would return home to cook your dinner and hope to end up in your arms once more. Not that night.

You called again and again, and I ignored it. When Robert from my chemistry seminar touched my thigh and pulled me against him, I let him, I laughed. Robert saw me. Robert could feel my hands on him. When he kissed me, I let it happen.

"You're beautiful," he said, slurring into my ear as we fucked against the wall of the smoking area.

People could see: over Robert's shoulder, I saw a man watching, a pair of girls sneering. Someone jeered something I couldn't hear. My phone buzzed in my jacket pocket. The music pounded in my head through the bricks. His hands squeezed my thigh; his chest crushed the air out of me.

And I laughed and laughed, because Robert's hands may as well have been made of papier-mâché. It was you I wanted. You. You. You. You. You.

*

That night I came back drunk and full of another man's cum. I found that you had locked me out of our house. My punishment for disappearing, for ignoring your calls, and leaving you to forage for your own dinner.

So I pounded the door. I took off my heels and kicked it as hard as I could. I screamed, and I laughed, and I yelled. I bounced pebbles from the driveway off our bedroom window until you let me in if only to avoid the spectacle.

The lights of our hallway were too harsh. Your face was stone. Your hands trembled. But your eyes were like a fire that burned cold. I feared it would put me out forever. I wanted to quake in terror, but instead, I laughed in your face, until your hand found my hair and you slammed me against the front door.

'Whore,' you called me.

You slapped me, and I fell on the scratchy doormat, cracking my head against our letterbox. I scrambled and kicked, but you pushed my face down with your foot. You crouched over me, ripping at my dress.

You yanked down my underwear and beat me bloody when you found that another man had beaten you to that place inside me.

You told me you'd make me wish I'd never been born. Then you violated me from behind, telling me that that other place was too dirty for you to use. When I tried to speak, when I tried to look at you, your fist came down on my head until there was blood in my eyes. My arms and legs ached. And I laughed because you were looking at me. You were looking right at me.

You were all mine again.

*

I finished my degree and graduated with those cold burning eyes on me. Busy and dedicated to your job you remained, but you never stopped looking my way. You'd return from work, and you'd come back and put your hands on me. Such strong hands.

You met Robert just once at my graduation ceremony. And it was like you knew. He came over to me, to congratulate me, to say goodbye. And you took a step between us and said that he had nothing to say to me, nothing at all.

I saw him leaving in his car, sporting a black eye.

How did you find out? I always wondered.

I suspect you'll always keep me wondering.

And yes, there were times you made me afraid. Once when my brother came to stay, you left to go and buy another bottle of wine. I was making dinner and Archie spotted a bruise on my wrist.

He asked me to come home with him; I never told you that. Did you notice his coldness to you after? How he stopped calling, stopped smiling, stopped laughing at your jokes. Or did you never see, because you had what you wanted from Archie by that point?

I told my brother that he had no reason to fear. I was devoted to you. How couldn't I be? You said you loved me. You couldn't keep away from me. Which is how I ended up twenty-two and pregnant.

I hadn't realised it before, but that was all I needed to do to make you mine and mine alone. Nights by my side, tending to my every need. Your rumbling laughter in my ear, your hands in mine. You even managed to wrangle it so you could work from home; you, who used to disappear with your dinner into your study without a word to me.

You were different when we became three. Do you remember how you used to rest your head on my stomach? How you'd whisper to our child? I remember how you told him how much we loved him already, you and I, how excited we were waiting for him.

Waiting and waiting and waiting.

*

You held Alex before me. I was bloodied and delirious, and you took him and held him in your big strong hands. You swamped him. I was frightened you'd rip him in two. I asked for him, broken as I was, I begged you, I remember that. And you looked right at me and pretended that you hadn't heard.

You took him from the room while I cried 'Let me see my baby,' over and over again until the pain became too much, too terrible, and I slept.

Do you know, I had nightmares for the longest time that you had lost him when you left the room. That maybe Alexander was not my real son. Only a mother would know, and you wouldn't let me see him. You handed him off to a nurse, who washed him, cleaned him, and muddled him with another child.

I'd wake in the night, frightened for months. I'd watch Alex sleep in his crib and try to see where his features met mine. Was he like me? Was he like you? It frightened me that I couldn't tell. It took me so long to be comfortable with our baby. And you did that to me.

Cruelty always came easiest to you. You know that, don't

you? It has always been so much easier for you to be cruel than kind.

*

It was six months before I could see that he was my child, after all. We share a common nose, the same ears, the same laugh. Six months and I could see it, and my heart was filled with love. I felt guilty that you had given me cause to doubt it. That my affection for our son was delayed.

But once it was there, it grew inside me like a forest. No longer bored and alone at home while you whittled away working. I barely noticed when you returned. At home, I had found my own little world with our son.

I had thought that I knew what love was before I became a mother. But I didn't.

With you, I'd have said that I'd do anything for you, that if it came down to it, I'd have thrown myself in front of a bullet for you. But it was just empty words. In truth, if someone had pointed a gun at you, I'd have run.

But with our son? No, for him, I'd have taken that bullet. For Alex, I'd rip flesh from bone, I'd gouge and maim. I'd kill. I never imagined myself as someone who could kill before I became a mother.

I'd sit there and watch him dribble on his bib or kick his tiny legs, how he'd clasp his little fist around a lock of my hair but never pull or yank. The feeling was so overwhelming that I would sometimes be reduced to tears.

You were jealous.

I laughed the first time I realised it. My big, strong, successful husband, jealous of his little baby son. The notion was utterly ridiculous. But once my body returned to normal, once I was myself again, you wanted me more than ever. You resented my wanting to sleep with our restless son in our bed. You begrudged me for occasionally sleeping in the nursery. You told me to ignore his cries as you laid me back on our bed.

You bruised my wrists holding me down as you took your time inside of me. You told me to look at you and just you.

You said I'd mess him up if I allowed him to be so clingy.

And when you were done with me, you laid your body over mine, keeping me in our bed as our son cried, and I wept soundlessly into the pillow.

*

You had the morning off, and we took him to school together. We had researched for a long time to find the right place. I was pregnant again. I kept nearly tearing up, and you kept shooting me looks when you thought Alex couldn't see us.

"Don't do this," you whispered to me. "Not today."

We took him to the front gates where the other kids played. He hugged my waist and hid his face in my skirt.

"Mummy..."

I clung to him and felt my face growing hot with tears.

Then you pulled him from me, clasping him in your arms and holding him high. You told him he was going to have loads of fun, much more than he would at home with silly old Mummy. You tickled him and made him laugh.

Then another little boy caught his attention with some brightly coloured, noisy toy, and Alex ran into school smiling.

As he went in, he looked back at me and said, "It's alright, Mummy!" before dashing away from me into that next chapter of his life.

And I wanted to be proud of our brave little boy, I wanted to feel ... good. But my heart broke. I waved and waved until Alex's class had gone inside, and you pulled me back to the car. You snarled at me on the way home, said I'd tried to sabotage Alex on his first day, the most important day.

And I cried. You said the new baby would soon occupy my time. You tapped my stomach like it was a table, impatient and uninterested.

Cruelty over kindness every time. Every damn time.

*

Soon, we had three children. It exhausted me. As soon as one was born, you were at me, big hands on my hips, tugging down my underwear, trying to put another baby in me. It drained the life out of me. There were days I'd look at my face in the mirror, bags under my eyes, my skin a mess. My breasts stretched, and my stomach lined. I was not your beautiful young wife anymore.

In between Moira and Jacob, I begged you to take a break; I said I wanted to bounce back. I was barely twenty-six and felt more like forty-two. Moira's birth had been painful, violent. They had to cut her out of me. And although I could never hate her for it, our darling little girl, I felt wrong in my skin after her. My scar made me feel ugly, like a corpse. You said yes. You acted sympathetic, sweet. You told me I was beautiful, that I was a wonderful mother, and that made me even more beautiful.

But on our anniversary, you had me in the cloakroom of the restaurant we were in. Your hand on my mouth. The two of us drunk on red wine and breathless with laughter, high on the fear of being caught. After, I realised that you hadn't used a condom like you told me you would.

In the taxi home, my thighs were sticky with you. I remember suggesting the morning after pill, just to cover ourselves. You looked at me with those cold eyes that burned like a distant star.

"No," you said. "There are lots of powerful hormones in that thing. No, I say we just let nature take its course."

That was how we ended up with three children before I was even thirty. You said that you always wanted a large family; you never asked what I might have wanted. You said we could afford it. You were a highly paid barrister, you said if the children exhausted me, I could always hire someone to help out.

That was your solution for everything. Toss money at it until it goes away.

You squandered my twenties, keeping me in a state of near-permanent pregnancy. You'd parade me around at those decadent parties with your firm—the trophy wife who had no career to discuss, no opinion you wouldn't talk over. Staring at the champagne I couldn't drink while you charmed and flirted, all the time with me on your arm. The *trophy* wife, squeezed into a dress, pregnant belly protruding, bloated like a sow, swollen feet burning in kitten heels.

You'd glance down at my flushed face, the self-conscious way I held myself as we stood facing the tiny, brilliant women of your firm, and you'd smirk.

You'd *smirk*. It was like you kept me pregnant to keep me slow and sore and vulnerable and trapped with you as the number of children we had increased rapidly.

We'd go to those parties, and I'd count the minutes where I wouldn't speak. Minutes became hours. Sometimes it would extend to the taxi ride home, where you would opt to talk on your phone while I sat beside you, tired and exhausted and bloated with our child inside me.

We'd go home, and I'd find myself watching your sleeping skull, and imagine drizzling it with hot acid. Then I'd slink out and go and watch our children sleep instead.

Alex, Moira, and Jacob.

The four of us had our own world that did not include you. You made that easy. You worked, and you worked, and then you'd come home to manhandle me away. You'd bark at our children and not even pretend to be embarrassed when they cowered in your presence.

There was a family photograph, taken before Chris was born. You and I sat on chairs in the living room. Me in my best dress, you in your suit. The children, who you had bought special new outfits for, were excited. Alex stood beside me with his hand on my shoulder, looking solemn, you told him that smiling made him look weak. Moira on my lap, red-eyed—you'd made her cry ten minutes before the photo was taken, you'd barked at her to stop sucking her thumb. Then little Jacob, only two years old, sat on your lap, still crying. He hadn't wanted you to hold him. He called for me and wept louder when you shook him hard to try and 'snap some sense into the spoilt little brat.' I begged you to stop. Alex said that Jake could come and stand with him instead. You insisted, and the embarrassed photographer took the picture anyway, tears and all.

You hung that photo above the mantle in the living room. I felt sick every time I looked at it.

When he was eight, Jake smashed the frame throwing a ball around the living room. I told you it was me and made excuses whenever you talked about having it re-framed.

*

You had Alex's life all planned out, without my input. He was just a little boy, but as soon as he turned six, he stopped being your child and instead became your project. Good marks and positive comments from his teachers after one year of school had him suddenly subjected to tutors, private schooling, and daily athletics. There was no *tired* for him. No fun, no rest, no days off. You told him that anything less than perfection was disgraceful and let himself and our whole family down.

I told you to leave him alone. We fought about it often. I'd still fight you about it now. It wasn't fair. He was just a little boy who wanted to make you proud.

You said I wanted to coddle him, make him weak, make him slow. My concerns were dismissed, you told me that I didn't know what was best for my own son.

I screamed at you, so then you grabbed my head in your big strong hands and squeezed until my eyes started to burn with tears.

"You're an empty-headed little fool!"

*

You sent him away when he was only eleven. A private school. You made the arrangements without telling me. I found out about it from Alex, who said miserably that he was nervous about boarding in case the other boys weren't nice.

I couldn't even reassure our son that he wouldn't be sent away.

"It's already done," you told me bluntly.

You knew I needed him. I needed him with me. He was my special boy. He helped me with Moira and Jake. He was just a child, but he understood how it was for me to love you and hate you at the same time. I felt better, safer, knowing he was coming home from school to me every day. I felt better knowing I could check on him at night, that he'd be in his room asleep and not somewhere far away.

You took him and sent him off to school in an instant, because once—just once—he stabbed you with a letter opener.

*

That day you were working from home. Typing away in your study, exchanging emails with Clara from marketing who left long dark hairs on your suits' collars for me to find and collect. Moira and Jake were playing, chasing each other through the hallway and up and down the stairs.

We bought this big house for our children, but you hated the sound of them playing. You hated it.

You put on loud classical music to shut them out. Then you left your study for a few minutes to badger me about dinner as I helped Alex with his homework. While we talked, Moira and Jacob moved their game of chase into your study. Jacob tripped and knocked his sister into your desk, spilling the coffee I had made for you all over the Newman papers and your laptop.

You found them.

Moira, you threw out into the hallway by her pinafore, you ripped the strap clean off in the struggle. I found her sobbing hysterically out there.

Alex started banging on the door over the sound of Mozart, your shouts, and Jake's screams for me to help him. I took to the door as well, kicking it as hard as I could, shattering the nail of my big toe. The pain would come later, in that moment, there was only panic. Then like a clap of thunder, a harsh slap and our son weeping. I kicked and bashed my fists until the deadbolt gave out. The door opened, and there you were, holding our child, our four-year-old child in your big strong hands as you struck his tiny face.

I didn't know what to do. I froze.

You'd never touched the children.

You'd never—

Alex dove at you, faster and angrier than I had the capacity to be in that moment. He hit you as hard as he could with his child's fists. You dropped Jake to the floor where he curled into the fetal position. Then turning back to Alex, you swatted him away as if he were a fly.

"Weak," you called him, "Mummy's boy."

But then you turned your back and reached for Jake again. Alex got up, I saw him go for your letter opener. I saw him clasp it in his hand. And I said nothing as he rushed at you and drove it into your back.

*

You were calm. You were calm in the ambulance, calm in the hospital. Alex was frightened, his hands trembled. He told you 'sorry' over and over again. But you were so *calm*. You told him quietly that it wasn't his fault, that he must have been afraid. You told him that you weren't angry with him.

You told him that a real man would do anything to protect his family. He cried, and you held him.

And I thought it might be alright, but then, just two weeks later, as your scar healed, you sent him away. I cried, and I pleaded. You said it was inevitable, it was done. You said it wasn't a punishment. You called me a child. You said I corrupted the children with my weakness, my hysteria.

But it wasn't like that at all.

You have such big strong hands, and you wanted to pummel the life out of me. You wanted to squeeze any essence of me out of our children. I'd never let you!

Never!

*

It took time. It took more time than I imagined, but I tricked the 'housekeeper' you hired to spy on me, to go to the shops one day. You were at work. I picked up Moira and Jake from school, I called the boarding school and explained that there had been a family emergency and that I would be collecting him at once.

Then with Moira and Jake in the back, I drove to get our son. The children weren't frightened—they weren't, they were sat in the back of the car, we were singing. Singing! They wouldn't have been singing if they were frightened, would they?

We collected Alex.

Nine months he'd been gone, nine—and already different, taller, colder. He had gone away with my features, my mannerisms. And nine months in that place, he walked over to me so much like you. His eyes were like yours, all fire and ice.

He hugged me when I rushed to him but said he wanted to sit in the back with Moira and Jake. He asked where we were going, and I realised that I wasn't sure. I suggested my parents' house because it was the only place I felt we could hide from you. I'd go back, and Mum and Dad would listen, and Archie would back me up.

I had to keep them safe from you.

We stopped for ice cream on the way, and as I paid, I heard the sirens. The police came and collected us. And at first, I didn't understand, these were my children. How could I not be allowed to go on a drive with my children? You were with them, red-eyed and frightened. Moira and Jake ran to you, and I was confused. How . . . ?

But of course, Alex had called you from the phone booth outside. You told me that he had been concerned. He had said I was frightening Moira and Jake.

But it wasn't true. It wasn't! It wasn't! I'd never! I'd never!

*

You locked me away for two months. Two months without a word of comfort from you, without our children, without your strong hands on me, without those cold eyes bright and burning.

I don't remember much from that time. Only my eyes ached from crying. My hands had to be tied down. I screamed myself hoarse. I wanted to see my children, I asked and asked, but nobody came. I screeched until my throat ached and nothing was left but pain.

But you never heard me. You never came.

You only let them release me in the end because it was there that they discovered I was pregnant with Chris.

*

You came to see me then. Do you remember? You got on your knees in my cell and reached for my hand. I cried so miserably, and you said, 'My darling, what's all this for?' And you held me and rocked me like a child while I wept for you to take me home. I told you I was frightened, I was so frightened here.

And it felt so good, so safe, to be back in your arms, for you to stroke my sweat-drenched hair, to kiss my forehead. I clung to you and asked for it to be like before.

"And it will be," you said, do you remember that? "As long as you're good."

*

For a time, we lived together in your apartment in Chelsea, not the house, you said that was wrong for now. You had the housekeeper-spy collect a portion of my things, some of my books—nothing problematic or potentially pessimistic—just the cheesy romance novels that your sister buys me every birthday for lack of knowing me at all. It felt strange to be without my things, to be away from our home. I hadn't realised that you owned another property.

You told me it was Penelope's, you bought it from her to be closer to the office. I tried not to let it bother me that you'd never said. You told me that you had the one time I brought it up.

"I told you at the time." So blunt, as if stating that my challenging it would result in words like 'hysterical' being tossed at me again. You would place these words upon me like shackles whenever it took your fancy. It was hard to know what to feel about anything; it was hard to know what I could express without it being regarded as an inappropriate thing to feel.

I hated you for what you did to our children—my children— while I was locked away.

You acted quickly, so much so that I suspect it had been your plan from the beginning. You removed the children from our home, sending them all away to school. You turned my nest upside down and shook it to pieces, trampling it apart. I couldn't go home because there was nobody to go home to. I started to cry when you told me, and you called me over-emotional. You held me in your arms and gently offered to call the doctor until I managed to cram my misery back inside me. Once suitably calm, you said it would be better like this, without stress, me and Baby Number Four needed rest and relaxation.

You let me talk to them on the phone. Or you did until I became distressed, or hysterical—you always decided when that was. It broke my heart to hear them ask after me, 'Mummy, Mummy, when are you coming home?' I'd feel tears burning in my eyes, and you'd take the receiver from me.

You were doing this to protect me.

Alex's calls were the worst. He'd talk to me like you or one of your friends from the firm. He'd ask about my health as though I were a stranger, a colleague in a lift, as though he didn't honestly care to hear my answer.

I tried not to hate you for keeping the four of us apart. I tried. You were doing all of this to protect me. You said so.

And you were true to your word. You let me see them, all

of them, when Chris was born. I woke up to find my babies gathered around my bed. Alex was smiling, playing with a tuft of hair on Chris's forehead. Moira and Jake rested their heads on my shoulders. You told me that I'd done so well.

We felt like a real family for the first time in a long time. I felt like we could make it work.

That it would be alright now.

*

Despite always wanting a large family, I don't think you were ready for fatherhood before Chris. Your temper was out of control. You treated our children like your regiment. You wouldn't bat an eyelid at reducing Alex to tears, to smacking Jake on the back of the head, or screaming in Moira's face.

And yet, you treated Chris like he was made of glass.

You changed nappies, you read stories, I even heard you singing to him once. You loved him in a way you just couldn't with the others.

Once, when Chris was two, you raised your voice to him, but when he cried, you crumpled and held him tight, comforting him so tenderly.

You resented his adoration of me, of course. You'd work from home to spend more time with him. Then you'd sulk when he'd shrug off your games and hugs and love, to sit with me as I tended to the flowers in the garden.

You wanted to set him up on your shoulders, and he'd shy away, reaching for me every time. Because you, my love, have such big, strong hands and to our tiny son, they were frightening.

*

I found out about your other woman when Chris was four. Alex, Moira, and Jake were away at school. I'd hired a sitter for Chris, paid her extra so she'd stay the night. I'd worn that red nightie you liked under a trench coat. It felt exciting, like the old days.

I'd taken a train into town and then a taxi. I showed up at the Chelsea apartment to surprise you.

She was sat on your sofa, reading through the case files, wearing your university sweatshirt. Only twenty-three, I found out later. I don't know if it was more or less insulting that she looked like me. Long blonde hair like mine. Similar features. She even had a mole below her left eye, just like mine. From a distance, in a blurry photo, she could have been me, a younger me. Did that make it hurt more or less? I can't tell. I can't. I can't tell at all.

I saw her and froze. Then she saw me and screamed for you. She clambered behind the sofa like a rat in a cage. Her eyes darted about like she expected me to fly at her with a knife. I stood there, heart thundering in my ears while she cowered and cried.

I suspect you told her all about your *crazy* wife.

I could see it there in her eyes.

You were cooking, you'd taken your tie off. I don't think you'd ever cooked for me, not once, not even when I was pregnant and exhausted by each and every step. You stepped out of the kitchen and between her and me.

You said, "Emma, it's alright," and she trembled from behind the sofa in tears.

Humiliated and shocked, my heart in my throat, I turned and ran.

Your footsteps thundered after me.

I thought for a moment, you'd come for me with gentle words, tell me it wasn't how it looked, that there was some chance this wasn't what it seemed.

But then you grabbed my arm and steered me towards you. I was crying, but then I looked up at you and saw that your eyes were cold and blank.

"Go home," you told me.

I wanted to grab you, hit you, slap you, bite you. I wanted to be the savage you'd told her I was. I wanted to raise hell. Mostly, I wanted you. I wanted you to touch me, to bruise me, hit me, even if you had no passion for me, even if you only wanted her, I wanted your hands on me. Your eyes burned me and my skin, my bones, my whole being ached with it, that sensation.

So I hit you, swiped at you with nails bared, weeping and hysterical.

You grabbed me and pushed me back into the wall, cold-eyed.

"Go home, I mean it."

Then you turned and walked away. You didn't look back. Not a second glance. I heard you telling her that everything was okay before you closed the door.

And I wanted to scream. You held me once with such big strong hands, and you used me up. You used me up. You took what you wanted and now . . .

*

We carried on like that for a time. I would pretend I didn't notice when you returned home later and later, and less. Our children were all away at school, all except Chris. But I knew you'd soon see to that.

Your sister came over, and I heard her talking to our son, sat on her lap by the fire.

"I bet you can't wait to go off to big school like your brothers," she said in that simpering sweet voice she does for the children.

"A bit," he said. "I like being in the garden with Mummy."

"He loves it out there," you said. "Show Auntie your green thumbs, Chris."

You laughed, and she pretended to fuss over how green they were.

"But school will be more fun than staying here with silly old Mummy," she said. "You'll make loads of friends, have adventures, and your big brothers will be there to look after you."

I came in, and Chris clambered down to come for a cuddle. And I saw the two of you smirking at me like you knew a secret I wasn't privy to.

*

It's sick what you do. You trick me, you tell me you love me. You hold me down and impregnate me like a breeding horse. You give me your children to raise and love. Then as soon as they grow up, as soon as they become interesting to you, you take them and change them. You take them from me and make them yours. You wipe me out like a stain.

They even look like you, too much like you now. All three of them. All but Chris. The three of them have cold eyes that can burn.

They don't look at me, won't look my way. They came back from school for summer, ready with plans and friends. You drove them home, three teenage strangers.

At that age where a mother's unconditional love is embarrassing, you said, when Jake twisted out of my hug, when Moira rolled her eyes at my stupid attempts to talk.

Cruelty over kindness, just like you.

Rejected.

First by you and now by them.

I sobbed my eyes out in private. I snuck into your study when you went out (likely to see Emma, the twenty-three-year-old legal secretary). I put on Mozart and cried miserably into one of the cushions, trying to crush the hysterical scream out of me.

Alex found me. He told me to stop. He pulled me to my feet and held me. Only . . . like you, he has such strong hands and such cold eyes.

I felt numb. Looking at our children made me feel numb.

*

At the end of the summer, you told me that you had enrolled Chris into the same school that turned Alex and Jake into clones of you. You told me as an afterthought before you left for work in the morning.

"Can you cancel it?" I asked. "He's six. He shouldn't be away from home yet."

You smirked at me and readjusted your watch.

Do you remember? I begged you, and you just stood there, readjusting your watch with that contemptuous smirk on your face. You used me. You took all that was ever good in me, and everyone just let you do it. Nobody protected me.

"It will be good for him," you said. "You suffocate the children here. He should be with other kids his own age."

I reached for you, and you sneered at me in such a way it made me stop.

"It will be good for you too," you said. "An empty nest at last. I thought you'd always wanted that."

*

I didn't hurt him. He wasn't frightened. He thought it was an adventure. We were going swimming in the sea. He was fine. He wanted to go. He even helped me with the map. A last little holiday before he had to go off to big school. It was going to be a lovely day.

I think I honestly meant that, at first.

But as Chris smiled and chatted cheerfully, eating his ice cream, I kept thinking about how you were going to take him away from me. You took the others. You have such strong hands—how else could I stop you from just taking and taking and taking until there's nothing left of me?

You used me up, took my life, gave me children to love and used them to chip away at me. And what next? What would you have taken next?

You have such strong hands, and I don't.

But I still managed to hold him under the water. He scrambled and struggled, but I was strong enough for that. But then some woman walking her dog saw me. She started screaming, started grabbing me. Others came. There were so many of them, wrestling me to the ground, pulling my hair.

And Chris came back up, spluttering and gasping.

They wouldn't let me hold him. They wouldn't let me touch him.

But his eyes—his eyes were wild and bright.

His eyes were just like mine.

*

The last time you touched me, you broke my nose. You came to see me in a legal capacity. I don't remember what we said. If we said anything at all. You took one look at me and the next, I was on the floor, and everything was red. The police came and removed you from the cell.

I was your wife, bloated and bloody on the floor, laughing and laughing until my bones ached.

You were my brother's handsome friend from university, my lover, my husband, whose eyes are cold but can burn.

And you have such strong hands.

DATE NIGHT

Ron says he has a tragic history with women. He goes through stages of blaming himself, of going on and on about where it all went wrong. How he drives the women in his life away with his attitude. Or, he rants and raves about women, how it's all their fault like the whole gender is conspiring to break him.

He talks about it at work, over lunch, at the bar, on the long commute home. Heck, he brought it up in a meeting once. As you can imagine, it gets more than a little frustrating. Initially, I felt sorry for the poor guy—I mean, it's tragic. He just wants someone to love him. Who wouldn't want that?

But when you hear him go on and on and on, day after day, about all the ones who got away, just unmoving, unending whinging. Well, even saints run out of patience and sympathy eventually, right? So one night, you find yourself sat opposite your co-worker in a bar, and you start hearing this noise—it's like a tearing, grinding noise? You have Ron to listen to, which is hard enough, and this gritty noise over the top of his words. You thought it was someone dragging a barstool along the beer-sodden floor, but it's not. And eventually, you clock on—that's your teeth!

This idiot is sat there, ranting on about the great lesbian agenda, and you're grinding your teeth in sheer frustration because this is all he talks about now.

This guy is so full of shit, and this dull, self-deprecating conversation just never ends.

And I can tell you the names of these ladies that Ron has loved and lost—more than names, I have details, intimate details—names that match the age, hair colour, eye colour, and smell, why she was so great, and things he misses about her.

Abigail, twenty-three, brunette, brown eyes, smells of orange blossom, and she had the prettiest smile in the world; Ron misses the way she used to say, 'Was everything alright with your dinner, sir?'—He didn't even date this girl. She was our waitress at the Christmas meal last year.

Hazel, twenty-seven, blonde, green eyes, wore musky perfume, very kind and great with kids; Ron misses holding her hand—this girl, he did date . . . for a month.

Ivy, twenty-five, black hair, blue eyes, smelled of clean bedsheets. She had an honest way of speaking; Ron misses watching her walk across to the photocopier—Ivy worked at our company for six months, and he never plucked up the courage to ask her out.

These women and all the others are precious angels in one conversation over bagels in the morning, then beasts full of flaws and depravity by midmorning coffee.

I wanted to be a good friend, but you have to understand, I was so bored!

One night, I just snap. I say to him, I say, "Ron, stop whinging—what good does it do? If you want to win this woman back, go and do something about. Just shut up already!"

The second it was out of my mouth, I had this immense feeling of regret in the pit of my stomach. *Oh shit*, I thought, *I can't exactly take that back.*

Only Ron doesn't react. He just goes quiet. He doesn't look mad exactly, but he is staring at me with this really blank expression on his face. Then he nods his head once, then twice.

"You know, man, you're absolutely right. You're absolutely right."

Then he got up and walked out of the bar, coat and briefcase trailing behind him.

I didn't hear from Ron that weekend. Usually, we'd end up meeting for a beer on Saturday night. But that weekend, nothing. Then on Monday, he skips onto the commuter train like a completely different man. He's combed his hair, got on a new suit, and he seems more relaxed than I've seen him in the five years we've worked together.

"Hey, Ron," I say. "Everything okay?"

"Couldn't be better," he says. "Life is so good, isn't it?"

And ... I mean, I don't know what to think. I know this won't last. Two-thirds of the women he's pined after over the years haven't even given him the time of day. Hell, Chrissie from marketing thought Ron was engaged to this one barrister he had actually only exchanged three sentences with, for all he went on about her. If I ask, he'll obsess. And it will be over soon anyway. No point in setting him off.

Only, a couple weeks go by, and Ron's spirits stayed high. He was a different man at work, positive, helpful, *cheerful*. I mean, it was good, but it just seemed a little too good to be true. Most nights, he would head straight home instead of joining me or any of the other guys for a drink. And when he did, he'd stay for one or two before dashing off like he had somewhere to be.

*

One night, it's just Ron and me again, we're on our second round, and he starts talking about this girl he's dating. Apparently, that night I told him off, he went to see Betty (this waitress he'd dated for a week but obsessed over for six). He'd waited outside the café where she worked to surprise her. He was trying to decide what to say when just like in a romantic comedy, he accidentally walked into the most amazing girl.

At this point, he just started gushing. It's all the usual stuff, the same old speech. This girl is beautiful, in a classic kind of way, and *so* cute, so cute she could pull off any outfit. She has this really pure sense about her. She's kind of quiet and shy but has a very straight forward way of speaking. And she has these big, gorgeous green eyes. Her hair is pretty short, but he has persuaded her to grow it out. She's professional too, a junior police officer, although she is taking a little break from that currently. I smile and say that I'm happy for him.

"I think she's the one, buddy," Ron says with this wistful, puppy-eyed smile on his face. It's a look that I've seen one thousand times before. But no matter, let him go on. Some people just can't be helped; let the guy be happy for now.

So another fortnight goes past, and Ron is still a loved up ball of sunshine. This girl really has been a good influence on him. On our walk to the train station after work, he suddenly lets out a gasp and dashes off into this little boutique on Edington Street. And I wait outside for him, baffled. Ron returns after five minutes with this dopey look on his face, and he's clutching this fancy little shopping bag.

"Sorry, I saw this scarf in the window, and it's like it was made for my girlfriend! Want to see?"

"No, no. I'm good, Ronnie."

The more I looked for it, the more I noticed that he was always picking up stuff like that, little trinkets of affection. One lunch break, I went out to grab a copy of the paper, and I spot Ron at the makeup counter of a department store. He was chatting with the salesgirl over a rack of lipsticks. A month ago, Ron couldn't have talked to some shop girl or any woman so casually. He'd get tongue-tied and then angry because he was so nervous. But here he was, chatting, laughing, and eventually, he came away with a lipstick.

"It's our one month anniversary, so I wanted to get her something special," he explained on the train home.

"Are you seeing her tonight?" I ask.

"Oh yeah, we live together."

Now *this*, I thought, he should have mentioned. He's never lived with a woman before, not ever. It must be really serious for them to get to this stage already. Hell, I couldn't be happier with my girlfriend, but I couldn't have moved in with her after just one month.

"Woah, when did this happen?"

"Recently," he said. "Real recently, I know it's soon, but when you know, you know, you know?"

Again, he's smiling this soppy, self-satisfied smile.

"So when do I get to meet this amazing girl?"

Ron just stared at me for a second, and then, seeming to recover, he said, "Of course, of course, you have to meet her. Why not come back to my place tonight?"

"Tonight? Are you sure she won't mind me dropping in unannounced?"

"No, no. She's a really laid back sort of person. Please, man, I want you to meet her."

So when we reached our spot, we got off the train and headed down the main street. We live about four blocks apart, so we usually go our separate ways when we reach the big bakery. I've been over to his place a handful of times, usually when we get turfed out of the bar. His apartment isn't all that different from mine. We both hate clutter, so it's a bare living room, kitchen, bath, and bedroom setup.

Ron was jangling his keys cheerfully on the walk over. The street lamps are never lit near his building. It can look a little spooky at night, especially as we have to walk these creaky metal stairs up the outside to get to Ron's. If someone else is coming down, you can't see them. You can only hear them. It's very ominous. Even I'll admit I don't like coming down here alone at night.

I waited patiently for Ron to unlock his door. It takes him ages to sort through his keys. He's always had more keys than me. Guess he must have a safe or something.

"Ah, here we are! Finally," Ron said, swinging open the front door. "Honey, I'm home!"

On stepping in, I couldn't help but notice the change since I was last here. The place is a complete mess. There are clothes and bags and things all piled up on the floor, leading from the hallway to the living room. There was one good seat on the sofa, but other than that, every square inch of the apartment was covered.

Guessing she isn't much of a cleaner bug. Not saying she has to be, but I always figured Ron was.

"Honey, hello? Hello!" Ron called. He chuckled to himself. "Oh, don't mind the mess. It's been so hectic around here as of late. Come on in, buddy."

I took off my shoes, leaving them by the front door, next to a box of neatly folded blouses and followed Ron through the narrow hallway towards the bedroom. Sighing cheerfully, Ron tapped on the door.

"Darling, are you decent?"

He opened it a smidge, peeked in and then swung it open. Stepping inside, I spotted her sat on a chair in the centre of the room.

Well, I say sat, actually she was bound to it. The woman in the chair, Ron was right, she really was a looker. Thick red hair growing just above her shoulders, creamy pale skin, bit of a nasty bruise on her forehead. Huge green eyes filled with tears, one of them blackened.

She was wearing one of Ron's baggy football shirts; it hung nicely from her frame, the sleeves finishing just above her elbows, or rather at the stump where her forearms and hands had been removed. The same with her long, thin legs, which cut off just below the knee. Thick ropes bound her tightly to the chair.

"Hi, beautiful," he said, bending down to kneel next to her. "Look what I picked up for you today at work. It's just a little present, but I picked it especially for you. Asked the lady at the store for some help." He produced the lipstick from his jacket pocket. "Happy anniversary, baby."

Her big, fearful eyes closed for a moment. She seemed to collect herself and then opened her eyes again. Her gaze was blank and cold.

"Want to try it on? I was told this sort of colour would be best for you." Ron unscrewed the lid and began to clumsily apply it to her trembling lips.

"Woah," he said, sitting back to admire his handiwork. "Wow, you look just, just beautiful, just perfect." He clasped his hands together, delighted. His smile quickly faded as she stared up at him, dead-eyed. Ron's lip curled in disgust.

"You ungrateful bitch!" His hand swung out, slapping her across the face. The blow was hard and sent both her and the chair clattering to the floor. "Fucking say thank you! Say thank you!" He stamped his foot down on her thin torso, producing a grunt of pain.

Ron yelled out, frustrated, and stamped down again and again.

"Ron, hey, buddy!" I reached out, grabbing him by the shoulders. "Ron, calm down! Like you said, like you said earlier, she's the quiet type! It's all okay!"

Ron took a deep breath, seeming to calm down. His shoulders were shaking in my hands.

"You're right, oh God, you're so right," he said. Ron rubbed his hands through his hair, exhaling heavily. "Baby, you just know how to push my buttons." He bent down to raise her and the chair back up. Her lipstick was smudged across her face, and her lip bleeding. "Poor thing, look what you made me do." He rubbed the blood away affectionately. "Good thing you were here, man. Hey, babe, this is one of the guys from the office. Say hi now."

She looked up at me, met my gaze for a second, and then quickly dropped her eyes back down to the floor.

"She is so shy, so ladylike," Ron said. He bent down to untie the ropes at the back. He lifted her delicately from the chair, letting her head rest against his shoulder. From this angle, I could see that her stumps were healing nicely.

"Let's go to the front room. I have some beers in the back," he explained. "You won't mind keeping my angel company for a few?"

"No, we'll be alright."

Ron placed her on the sofa's one good seat, between two piles of clothes. I opted for one of the metal chairs resting against the wall. Ron kissed her forehead, waving loftily as he stepped out towards the back room.

The two of us didn't speak for a few moments. I was trying to find the best way to sit and not overbalance the stack of books propped against my chair. They all seemed to be love advice books like, 'How to talk to women.' Guess Ron doesn't need these anymore. I gave up trying not to overbalance the books as they gave way, spreading across the floor. I looked up at her with a smile.

"Guess you're not much of a housekeeper, are you?"

I only meant it as a joke, but her eyes welled up with tears. Then she said in a tiny little voice, "Please, help me, please."

I blinked. "Erm, sorry, what did you say, sweetheart?"

Then Ron appeared from the backroom with a six-pack. Her eyes fell, hardened but blank.

"Did you guys talk about me?" he asked playfully. He handed me a beer before shifting one of the piles of clothes out of the way and curling up next to his girlfriend.

"Oh yeah," I said. "But you're right, Ron, she really is quiet."

"I hope you didn't tell her any stories of my exploits," he said, chuckling to himself.

"No, no, you're safe there. Hon, your boyfriend's a real great guy, a real stand-up guy." I settled back into my chair, taking a sip of my beer.

"You don't mind me drinking, do you, baby?" Ron asked, slipping an arm around her shoulder, his hand trailing down to meet her stump. She flinched when he touched the thin, reddened skin that covered the bone. Then she meekly shook her head. Ron kissed her hair.

"So, Ron tells me that you're taking a break from police work?" I tried.

She looked like she hadn't heard the question. Her eyes were cloudy, her chin pressed against her chest.

"Oh yeah," Ron said, cutting in. "I don't like the thought

of my girlfriend doing something like that. Anything could happen to her."

"Definitely, it's a dangerous world out there."

"She isn't much of a housekeeper, but we both feel safer with her here," Ron explained.

He started going on about something—cooking for two, how happy they were together. His girl's eyes got all misty and red again.

Being in love can be pretty overwhelming, I suppose?

I just kept noticing the way the joint of her knee curled into nothing. I wondered what he used to make the cut.

"You know, man," Ron said brightly. "I never would have plucked up the courage to meet a woman like her if not for your pep talk that night at the bar."

Ron squeezed her shoulder gently. "Babe, I don't like to kiss and tell, but I did have a past before you, chased a lot of the wrong women."

"Got to break a lot of eggs, Ron, buddy," I said, chuckling.

"No, seriously. You made me realise what's important. Baby, you should say thanks to my friend here. It's him you have to thank for our domestic bliss."

And you know? It was the weirdest thing. For a second, she was looking at me with real anger in her eyes, like she wanted to hurt me.

"Ron, your happiness means the world to me."

But he was frowning. He glared down at her.

"Baby, say thank you. You're being rude."

If anything, her jaw looked locked up tight.

"Don't be rude. Say thank you!"

"Ron, the little lady has gone shy."

"Yeah, yeah, but it wouldn't kill her to say fucking thank you for once—for this! Would it kill you?" He grabbed her face, squeezing her cheeks hard. "Would it fucking kill you?"

Her voice hardened as she muttered, "Don't know. Would it?"

There was a pause. Ron's eyes met mine. Then we started

to laugh. I remember how the tears brimmed in my eyes as I laughed. How Ron doubled over, slapping her on the back. How that sent her awkwardly toppling onto one of the piles of clothes.

That set us off laughing again. How we laughed and laughed as pairs of socks and packets of underwear rolled around on the floor. As I downed the last of my beer, Ron sat her back upright, still catching his breath.

"Ron, I have to head off. The missus will be worried. But this has been so much fun," I said, getting to my feet.

"Sure thing, thanks for coming round." Ron got up, clasping my hand firmly and shaking it. "We should get together, the four of us sometime, for dinner or something?"

"I'd love that. And it was lovely meeting you, sweetheart. Look after Ron for me; he's one of the good ones." She didn't reply. She just stayed where Ron placed her, those cold green eyes on the floor.

Ron stood, waving from the front door as I descended the creaking metal stairs.

On my way home, I couldn't help but feel a little proud.

A few months ago, I would have avoided coming back for a beer like the plague. It was usually an invitation that involved an evening of listening to Ron whinge and then sat awkwardly while he cried into some previous flame's nightdress. But look here, he actually took my advice!

And she seems great! Bit on the quiet side, but great. He's a changed man and so happy. I guess there really is someone out there for everyone.

As I climbed the steps to my own apartment, I almost wanted to pat myself on the back. No more listening to Ron's whinging every day. This will improve my commute completely! I'm glad for the guy. I mean, who doesn't want to be loved?

I slipped the key into the front door.

"Honey, I'm home!"

THIRTEEN

"I want to kill myself."

The first time he told me that he burst into tears. I tried to calm him down, I told him how much we would miss him if he did, how much I loved him, how much we all loved him.

"Peter, you're so young," I told him, "You're so young, you don't know anything yet. So, don't talk like that."

I wanted him to feel better, but after that he kept saying that he wanted to kill himself. Peter had kept it quiet for so long and once the words reached the surface, they dripped from him like water. He'd say it every day, he'd say it no matter how much it hurt our parents, no matter what was happening in the family. He'd say it with this distant look on his face.

He said it to the point it began to feel ridiculous to me.

Mum would ask him to clean his room and he'd say, "What's the point?"

She would roll her eyes and respond, "What do you mean what's the point? Don't you want to help out around here?"

And he'd say, "No, I really, really want to kill myself."

He stopped going to school. He stopped seeing his friends. He would sit in his bedroom in front of his computer, lazily playing video games or watching old episodes of some mindless tv show. He'd stay up all night just to see the sunrise before starting the same cycle over again. On other occasions, he'd just sleep endlessly. He stopped washing. He stopped brushing his teeth. He stopped smiling or looking people in the eye. He didn't listen when people talked to him.

And when he did speak, it was always the same, 'I want to kill myself.'

Then one night we had a fight. Mum and Dad had gone away, and I was left alone with him. He was depressing me, so I went out to a party. I drank too much and came back to find the house a mess. He'd been there alone. Dirty dishes, boxes and paper littered the counter-tops, pizza boxes, receipts, and empty cans.

"What the fuck is this?"

"If you don't like it, you can clean it."

"You're so lazy."

I loaded the rubbish into a bag, shaking with rage.

"Hey, it's only bothering you, so you can clean it up." He tossed another empty can onto the floor where the brown remnants leaked out over the carpet.

"You don't even care how miserable you're making everyone," I snapped at him.

"What?"

"You don't care about anyone but yourself!"

"You can't say that to me! You know! You know what I'm going through!" He was shaking. The tears came easy then, dripping from his chin and onto the sodden carpet. "I want to kill myself!"

I laughed in his face. "Don't you dare keep throwing that at me! Don't you dare!"

He didn't reply, he just stared at me, stunned, his eyes red from crying.

His voice came out small. "What?"

"You know what you're doing! Threatening me with it whenever things don't go your way! It stops now! God, will you just grow up?"

"I want to kill myself," he said miserably.

"Oh, you just stop it! You stop it!" I yelled. "You're pathetic! Nobody cares!"

He was still for a moment, stunned.

I snorted in disgust and turned my back.

"You fucking bastard!" He snarled at me, he lunged forwards and shoved me into the wall. "Fuck you! You're so fucking selfish! You're so fucking! You don't give a shit! You don't give a shit!"

My fists flailed out in front of me, and I hit him across the jaw as he hit me in the stomach. We fell away from each other, too stunned to speak at first.

But then I screamed at him to get out and he did.

That was the last time I saw Peter.

*

The policeman is dead-eyed, vacant and unsympathetic. I suppose that is a side effect of the job. Mum has always cried loudly, she does it during sad advertisements about pets on tv, but this is worse. It almost embarrasses me. Me, who can scarcely make a sound.

But this guy doesn't ever change his expression from dull and blank and empty.

He asks questions like he's reading off a script. He waits patiently while Mum chokes on her words and breaks down again and again and again. Dad gives short, brief, and to the point answers. He occasionally snaps, "You're upsetting my wife!" while Mum shakes her head and tries to compose herself.

They have ruled out suicide and tell us, disturbingly, that Peter was killed by someone after he left the house angry and hurting that night. I'm not privy to the facts of his murder. My parents were told in hushed voices at the police station and neither have been able to share the details with me.

There was one phrase I heard before the door was closed in my face—"the body showed signs of a struggle."

I know it was violent, savage. I know that Peter died afraid and in a lot of pain. I know that Mum freezes up whenever she talks about it.

Mostly, I know that it is all my fault.

My parents know it too. Mum won't even look me in the eye. The three of us sit in a room together with the blank-faced, dead-eyed detective and it's like there is an entire world between us.

I've explained about our argument, my frustration with him. I know it shocked Mum and Dad. I sounded too angry. I want to let go of that, to stop being angry with Peter for his constant threat of suicide. I want to feel sad that he's gone. But all I am is angry. I'm so fucking angry with him. I've had this pain in my stomach still from where he hit me. I can hardly breathe. Every time I sit up I feel it, and I get angry all over again.

How could he do this?

I think about his sullen eyes, his scowl, his unwashed hair. I want to grab him and scream in his face. I want to go back and yank his hair when he tries to leave the house that night and shove him onto the floor. I imagine myself raining punches down on him, telling him that I love him, that I love him so much and so does Mum and Dad. I see myself calling him stupid, calling him the fucking worst. He cries and I cry and I tell him that when he hurts himself, he's hurting me. He clings to me and says he'd never hurt me.

But then I open my eyes and Peter is gone, and I am still here and then it hurts too much to try and imagine otherwise.

*

I wander the streets at night a lot. Mum cries herself to sleep, she wakes up in the night and the crying starts again. Dad sits up, awake. I know he sees me leave the house. He watches me from the window, but he doesn't try to stop me, he doesn't ask in the morning as we sit together drinking coffee.

I roam the streets and walk the route he walked the night he died. I follow the road past the bus stop, past the little red houses. I walk up the hill, over the bridge, and sit for a time, watching the late-night train speed underneath.

I watch the park where he was found from a distance.

Most nights it's quiet, void of anything, the swings catch in the wind, and the rusty hinges shriek. Other nights a gaggle of drunks wander this way, staggering, falling against the swings. Sometimes they try and get on, flailing around like large drunken toddlers, but on others they just carry on walking home. They never notice me up on the hill, watching them.

I wonder sometimes if one of them was the one who killed Peter. They don't look like the type. These are red-faced family men; they look like Dad. But still, I imagine Peter, upset from our argument, storming down here, sitting on the swings, trying to calm down. I imagine these men, red-faced family men, stumbling drunkenly into the park.

They try and talk to him, like banter in the pub, just kidding around. And he is in no mood for it. He tells them to fuck off. And they change, they get hostile, they tell him to mind his fucking manners. They tell him to apologise and he won't. He never apologises. One of them—the one with the big, red nose, I've decided—gives him a warning, calls him *boy*, maybe he shoves him. And Peter just sneers and calls him something bad, like a miserable, drunk old bastard. That's when one of them, the one with the big, red nose, punches him in the face. The blow sends him toppling against the slide, the sharp metal edge cracks the side of his head. The men panic and leave and forget.

Sometimes I think about walking down the hill and asking them why they did it. Why did they hurt Peter? He was just a stupid, selfish idiot. They didn't have to kill him over it.

At other times, I know that's not what happened. These are red-faced family men, they look like Dad. And they don't always stop here, some nights they just carry on walking home.

I watch them walk home, and eventually, I go home as well. I follow the route he never made it down. I go over the bridge, up the hill, down the road past the little red houses and the bus stop and all the way to my house. Dad has managed to go back to bed. My mother is asleep, and I return to silence.

Then I stay up, just to watch the sunrise.

When I do sleep, I see Peter sat at the top of a hill, his clothes all red. He watches me and when he opens his mouth to speak, I hear the rush of a train cutting through the engine, tearing the ground apart. In my dream, I cover my ears and beg him to shut up. But then he closes his mouth again; the silence is too strong, too painful, and I weep for him to talk to me once again.

*

We haven't seen the detective for a few days now. His presence hangs over the house like a dark cloud. Dad stays in the garden, he tends to the flowers and keeps his lawnmower company. Mum stays on the sofa for a while, always crying. She can't enjoy her books, she can't enjoy her favourite tv shows. She asks what kind of mother lets this happen to her child. She closes the door in my face when I try to comfort her.

After a while, she goes to Peter's room with the intention of sorting through his belongings. I hear her upstairs, moving things, going through his wardrobe. Then silence. I find her curled up on his bed, clinging to a teddy bear he kept when we were small. Her whole body shakes from crying. And I want to tell her that I'm sorry. But I'm so angry with him for letting her cry that I can't muster one word before she closes the door.

She doesn't do any more sorting. She stays in his room all night, and we hear her crying through the door. Dad stands outside the room but doesn't manage to go in. We bump into each other in the corridor, and he walks away when I open my mouth to speak.

*

I go out at night and sit up on the hill that overlooks the park where they found him. I would go to the sea or the sky, I would go anywhere that isn't that house.

I sit up there, where he was in my dream. I lie back and feel the cool ground beneath my fingers. I imagine the red-faced men returning and hurling rocks and stones at them, demanding they tell me about the night he died. I know they know nothing, I know they have nothing to do with it. But Peter is gone, and I'm desperate to blame someone else.

The men don't come, and I feel my insides ache at the thought of walking down the hill, back to that silent house.

When I look up, I stare down and I imagine Peter at the bottom of the hill, his sullen eyes, his unwashed hair. For that moment, he seems so real to me that I could reach out and touch him if I'd just step forwards. Peter only stands there staring at me. I grab a handful of dirt and throw it at him.

"I hate you!" I yell at him. "You're so selfish!"

The dirt hits his chest and leaves a scattered brown stain on his grey t-shirt.

Then he takes a step towards me.

I stumble and fall backwards, hitting the ground hard.

"What?"

Peter is climbing the hill towards me, one step at a time. His expression blank, eyes never leaving me. I open my mouth to speak as a train comes rushing past the park, drowning out my words, drowning out my frightened gasp. The train passes us by, and Peter is still climbing the hill towards me.

So, I stagger to my feet and run. I run over the bridge and down the hill. I can't see the top of the street, where the bridge comes out. I rush out into the road, to try and see if he's following me. I hear the screech of a horn, lights flash, and I leap to the pavement on the other side of the street, narrowly missing the lorry that speeds past.

As I catch my breath, I tell myself that I'm tired, that I haven't really slept since the night he died, but then I spot him at the top of the hill. He's walking slowly towards me. He isn't angry. I want him to be angry. I want him to be sad. I want something from him that isn't just empty.

"Go away!" I scream at him. "GO AWAY!"

I want him to feel something.

But his expression doesn't falter. He opens his mouth and I hear the thudding of the train, the whirring of wires, the whump of the engine. And I scream for him to shut up, to stop it, and to leave me alone. But all of my words are drowned out by the screech of wheels, the blaring of the horn. I drop to my knees and I cover my ears until that awful sound goes away.

As I look up, Peter is right in front of me. His expression is void and empty, but his eyes are streaming with tears.

"Stop following me!" I yell at him. "Stop following me, you selfish prick!"

I reach up to hit him again. I can see the bruise on his cheek from where I smacked him the other day. But he opens his mouth, and the sound of the train comes louder and more ferociously than before. It's too much, and I scream out in fright, staggering back from him.

So I run. I scramble over to the other side of the road towards little white houses, towards town and the police station. I keep running, stumbling and afraid, until that awful sound is gone. But every time I so much as glance over my shoulder, Peter is still there, walking just behind me like a shadow.

"Stop following me!"

I throw a stick at him, it bumps against his shoulder, but he keeps coming.

"Leave me alone!"

Every time I try to speak, every time I try to fight, he opens his mouth, and the train comes rushing at me, cutting through the dark and hammering me to the ground. So I run, blinded by tears, heart pounding in my chest.

I turn a corner and trip and fall onto the ground, bashing my knees. I see him coming around the corner after me, and I burst into tears.

"Peter! LEAVE ME ALONE! LEAVE ME ALONE!"

I grab a brick and hurl it at him. The brick passes right through his arm as though it never made contact. In a flash, he is closer to me than before, inches from my face. I raise my hands to protect myself, to push him away. His fist comes up and strikes me hard in the stomach. I fall and curl up in fright on the ground and, I remember, I remember . . .

Then I remember a past where I go after him. Where I follow him beyond the red houses, up over the bridge and up the hill. I find him sitting in the park, feeling sorry for himself. I imagine that we argue, that he tells me to leave him alone. I imagine him trying to leave the park, pushing past me. I see myself grabbing his unwashed hair and yanking him back onto the ground. I see myself raining punches down on him. I tell him that I hate him, that I hate him so much, I hate his whole selfish attitude. I tell him that nobody would care if he were gone. He is crying, and I'm crying too. I hit him until he bleeds. He doesn't hit me back. He just tries to cover his face. Eventually he doesn't move. And I go home and forget.

"I'm sorry!" I sob. "I'm sorry!"

But his face never changes. He stands a few feet in front of me, hands by his sides, still and quiet.

"Please leave me alone! Please, please, God!"

But he doesn't. He just stays there until I get up and try to walk away. I keep walking into town, my heart heavy in my chest. I walk down the back streets, past the red-faced family men moving from one pub to the next. I just keep walking, only looking back to check over my shoulder.

He's still there, following me.

"You broke our family," I tell him.

But Peter makes no sound now. He dogs my every step, hanging from me in every strip of street lamp light. I try and call out to him, and he just watches me with that horrible still expression while tears stream down his cheeks.

"Please don't cry," I tell him. "Peter, please, don't cry. I don't know what to do."

He walks towards me. I keep going because I don't want him to be close. I don't want him to reach out and touch me. I'm scared if he touches me, I'll forget to be angry, I'll forget to be sad. I'll just forget, and he will still be gone, and everything in me will be taken too.

I walk and as I do, I remember a time when we were small. Mum and Dad took me to a forest on the other side of town. We

found a clearing at the centre and we laid down, staring up at
the sky through the trees. We described the shapes the clouds
made. Dad was always bad at it; we would describe dragons and
castles and giraffes, he would describe the clouds as 'blob-like'
or 'a dish cloth.' I laughed so hard my ribs hurt.

I walk there again now, because I can't think of anywhere
else to go. I want to take him to the woods where he was once
so happy. Maybe then he'll leave me alone and just stay there,
quiet. I go through the town centre, past rows of shops and
houses. Through the bad side of town, up the big hill by the
rubbish tip. The smell makes me gag, and I cover my nose.
Peter is unphased and just keeps walking.

We reach the edge of the forest, and he hesitates before we
enter.

"You've followed me this far," I call after him.

But he doesn't follow.

So, I enter the forest alone, and for the first time, I feel him
rip away from me, just like before. When did the two of us get so
far apart? I want to ask him, but I know he won't answer.

The woods are dark, and it's hard to navigate. The footpath
seems to fade into the darkness of the shrubbery. My feet
crunch along the path, and I'm angry at him for staying on the
outside. Now he chooses to leave me on my own? An owl hoots
up ahead, growing louder and louder. The trees close together
and animals rustle out of sight and away. Something darts past
my shoe as it connects with the dirt of the footpath. I hear the
fear in my voice and stumble, crashing into a tree. I look around
for Peter, but he really is gone.

He's gone. He's gone, and I never really thought I'd know
what to do if he ever—!

I start to run, there is a tiny light up ahead, coming through
the trees. Then the rain starts to fall, crashing down onto the
ground, onto the trees and the plants, and it pounds against
my head like a drum. I trip and fall hard onto the wet, muddy
ground. My body aches, and I stumble, trying to get to my feet.
I scream for Peter, and it is lost under the sound of the rain. I

can't see. The moon goes behind the clouds, and I am left alone in the dark.

For the first time, I'm not angry with him. I am afraid, and I am sad.

I never wanted you to die. I'm sad. I'm so lonely without you that it hurts to breathe. I sit up and watch the sun rise because I can't believe that it can rise on a world without you in it. I'm so sorry I didn't protect you better. I'm sorry. I'm sorry, Peter, I'm sorry!

How can I exist, how can Peter exist without a shadow?

*

"I want to kill myself."

The first time I said it out loud, I burst into tears. I remember trying to calm down, tried to tell myself how many people would miss me if I did, how much my parents loved me.

"Peter, you're so young, and you don't know anything yet, nothing proper. I just . . . need to pull myself together."

I wanted to feel better, but after that I kept thinking it, I kept imagining it every second of every hour. I'd kept it quiet for so long and once the words reached the surface, they dripped from me like water. I'd say it every day, I'd say it no matter how much it hurt my parents, no matter what was happening in our family. I'd say it to the point it began to feel ridiculous to me.

Mum would ask me to clean my room, and I'd say, "What's the point?"

She would roll her eyes and respond, "What do you mean what's the point? Don't you want to help out around here?"

And I'd say, "No, I want to kill myself."

I stopped going to school. I stopped seeing my friends. I would sit in my bedroom in front of the computer, lazily playing video games or watching old episodes of some inane tv show well into the early hours of the morning. I'd sleep through the day. I stopped washing. I stopped brushing my teeth. I stopped smiling or looking people in the eye or really talking to anyone.

Then one night, my parents went away, and it was just me

alone. I tried to make an effort, I went out with friends, drank too much, I forgot about it all for a few hours and came back to find the house a mess. Dirty dishes, boxes and paper littered the counter-tops, pizza boxes, and receipts, and empty cans.

So, I went for a walk, I staggered down the street, past the bus stop and the little red houses. I climbed the hill, went over the bridge, and sat at the top of the hill staring down at the park. I thought about going there when I was little, my father pushing me on the swings. I thought about going to the woods on the other side of town and seeing dragons in the clouds with my mother. Then I thought about what a big fucking disappointment I must be to both of them. I thought about how dejected and sad they looked when they saw me. How much I must let them down.

I thought about how much better off they'd be if I just didn't exist anymore.

I waited until the late-night train was due. I walked past the park, had a little go on the swings, listened to the way they screeched from the rust one last time. Ignored the red-faced family men who stumbled through, being silly, joking around, wanting to try and squeeze onto the slide. I climbed over the fence and out onto the train tracks.

*

The darkness clears and I make my way through the woods and into the clearing at the centre. I lay down on the cool ground and stare up at the sky through the trees. The dark sky is dissolving into shades of purple and orange. The pain in my stomach is gone. I lie there and listen to the sound of the forest waking up. The last of the rain falling from the trees. I breathe in and out slowly, controlled. The clouds are forming above me, a dragon, a tree, and I guess, a dish cloth too.

I lie back and take in the view as the sun starts to rise.

CROCODILE TEARS

Your parents split when you were twenty-one, so you couldn't blame your personality on their divorce. You weren't that shocked. You had long come to understand that your image of a *happy family* did not match everyone else's. I mean, come on, nobody was ever going to whack your parents—screaming at each other from opposite ends of the dinner table—on a Christmas card.

They both moved on seamlessly.

Your mum started internet-dating. The less you knew about that, the better.

Your dad met a woman through work. In a whirlwind romance that your girlfriend referred to as a *classic mid-life crisis*, the two of them were living together and married before your graduation that year.

You pictured a wicked stepmother character, a 26-year-old peroxide blonde desperate to steal your dad's middle-management salary. But she was fifty-nine with 90s blonde highlights, wore 'Mum jeans,' and came with a daughter about your age with your exact same name. Lou and Lou.

They tell you that she went to boarding school but always lived in the same town. You struggle to imagine her, this girl, this woman, Other Lou, that the two of them insist is *just like you*. Your dad and his new wife reassure you that the two of you would get on like a house on fire.

But it felt weird, a new sister at twenty-one, so you held off meeting her until the wedding.

This was your introduction.

The first time the two of you met, she was aloof, laid-back, drifting lazily into the conversation with a one-liner every now and then. She surveyed you with a bored expression and sighed grey smoke circles into the sky. She was the cooler of the two of you, *undeniably*. Perfect silvery hair piled up onto her head, in a pale blue Grecian dress that hung from her slim shoulders. Black combat boots, a cigarette, and a hipflask put your pinching heels and too tight floral dress to shame.

"Little Lou," she calls you, and suddenly everyone is doing it.

The second time you met, she was more approachable, the life of the awkward little dinner party in your dad's new house. She told jokes, stories about her crazy friends, her stupid boyfriend. That time she was the leading lady, rather than the sarcastic supporting cast. You swapped numbers and took a drunken selfie together after your respective parents had gone to bed.

After that, it started properly.

The two of you become close.

She tells you about some guy who broke her heart when she was young and naïve. Fights with her dad. A violent drunk who she hates as much as she loves. She is an avid storyteller. Even her trips to the supermarket are comedy gold. She is always the hero of these stories, too cool for any bullshit.

She tells you that she's excellent at making friends but so, so bad at keeping them—she can't *deal* with dramatic people. Sometimes she shows you pictures of them, the friends she used to have. She points out the bad hair, the big noses, the awkward fashion choices. One of them, May, who she particularly despises now, has a punky, shaved head and a pierced nose. The two of them have their arms around each other's shoulders, laughing.

As close as sisters.

The closeness between the two of you seems real for a while. You shop together—you're desperate to low-key copy her Stevie Nicks shawls—she wants to be able to wear heels as effortlessly as you. You go for drinks. You have each other's back. You put down the perverted old men in the pubs and bars. You try your best not to roll your eyes when she refers to herself as an 'alpha female.'

You meet her boyfriend. He is quieter than you expected, ironic t-shirts, talks eagerly about video games until she drunkenly tells him that nobody gives a shit what he says. He looks embarrassed but accepts it, shrugging and rubbing his shaved head.

*

Your girlfriend isn't impressed by her. Lisa frowns at her abrupt manner, the way she ironically dismisses people. The first time the three of you hang out, Lisa sneaks off to the toilet to play Candy Crush on her phone, waiting for the hours to pass.

"She's weird," Lisa says. "Do you believe half the shit that comes out of her mouth? I hate that she always calls you 'Little Lou,' so patronising! Also, why are you wearing the same dress?"

Every time it comes up, you shrug it off. You never tell her that you and Lisa had a fight about her, of course. She would enjoy that too much. For someone who insists on her hatred of *dramatic people*, she lives for drama in real life. She has often referred to her parents' divorce as 'the greatest show on Earth.'

As time passes, your new sister starts to wear on you.

She turns into someone else when she has an audience. She enters a social gathering as a mirror that mocks everything in front of it. She talks over you and sneers at your attempts to return the favour. You don't take it personally; nobody is safe from her scorn. Her boyfriend gets it the worst. Nights out spoilt by fighting, with her telling him he is embarrassing or loud, or more drunk than anyone else.

It isn't always fun to be around. You develop a thick skin to wash it off when she hurts your feelings.

In reality, it would be easy to hurt her back. Her tough exterior is man-made, and it is painfully clear that she hates herself. She calls herself an alpha female but shrinks away in a crowd. A small gatherings person, desperate to cope in a bigger pond. You've watched her dish out terrible romantic advice and smirk like a wise old sage after. And her tall tales, the stories that impressed you so much when you first met, become funnier still, but not in the way she wants. She didn't *think* she saw Johnny Depp one week in Leicester Square, she *did* see him, AND he told her she was pretty. She tells you, bold as brass, that she's outraced Jaguars in her little Nissan Micra, and gotten away from police cars on the motorway.

The lies get bigger and funnier, and you and Lisa play a private drinking game when she talks—one sip for the inconsistencies, down your glass for a ridiculous lie etc.

At three different parties, you hear three different versions of the day her dad left. None of them include the fact that she ran after him into the street. And not even the amped-up movie script version includes the fact that he hit her.

Lisa thinks she's ridiculous, but ultimately you feel sorry for her. You don't bite back hard when she comes at you with a cruel barb. Your pity is noticed and not appreciated.

You realise that this was probably when she started to despise you.

*

You drift apart after you graduate and move to Liverpool for a job you hoped would be the *one*. She moves in with your parents and works in a shop that sells second-hand DVDs and video games. Her boyfriend comes to visit, but she visits him more. She doesn't say it, but you see that she is terrified of being alone, without the validating gaze of someone who loves her.

Lisa considers this a close save. She delights in telling your new Liverpool friends about your crazy bitch stepsister who was trying to *Single White Female* you. She bitches about her to anyone who has a minute. It gets boring. Your relationship with her does not last another year.

Your job deteriorates not long after. You show up late. You make mistakes. Eventually, you hand in your notice just to avoid the inevitable.

*

It is after the breakup with Lisa that your sort-of sister contacts you out of the blue. Bitterly, you suspect this is just because of her need to be around people she considers less fortunate than herself. You likely deserve it. I mean, look at you.

You're single, you're broke, you're unemployed. You're randomly still living in Liverpool. You've gained eight pounds since your breakup, and everyone thinks Lisa was the one who broke up with you.

On the other hand, your sort-of sister is in a dedicated, four-year relationship. She has a new wardrobe, she has gotten a proper, professional, well-paying job in London. She's even shaved the side of her head and looks like a punk-rock princess.

She comes to you eager to flash her cash and brag about her recent weight-loss. The two of you are friends again. You go drinking, she tells you about the guy in her office who really, really fancies her.

It grows tedious quickly, so you ask about her old friend May, who you remember, lived in that same city.

"Do you see her often?"

"Not really," she says vaguely. "I wouldn't be surprised if she is avoiding me. I could go my whole life without seeing any of those jerks again."

Three former friends she treats like evil exes.

There was May, her best friend from university, with the punky hair, who took no shit from anyone, who won a big cash poetry prize. She tells you that May was full of herself and turned everything into an argument.

Then there was Claudia, her friend from her misspent teenage years in the down-town leisure centre, painting sets for amateur dramatics groups. Claudia who smoked like a chimney and dominated the conversation through sheer charm. You knew Claudia too. She was two years above you in school. Your first kiss in a game of spin-the-bottle. You hear she went travelling abroad after uni.

Then there was Sabrina, her best friend from boarding school, with waist-length red hair like the Little Mermaid. Painfully intelligent and, according to *her*, so dull it was like watching a dishwasher whenever she opened her mouth.

"What do you reckon you'd do if you saw her? May, I mean?"

"I dunno. Push her in front of a bus, maybe?" she says.

A beat.

She laughs.

You laugh too.

Look at the two of you, laughing.

It's a joke.

"What did you two finally fall out over again?"

"She was jealous of me and boring. She was the most argumentative person in the whole world." She offers you a beer and settles back into the sofa. "Forget about it, Little Lou. Let's get you out of fucking Liverpool."

*

You always admired that about her. Her can-do attitude.

You feel lucky to have her in your life, leading you along to transform into something less embarrassing.

You get interviewed at the company where she works for an entry-level position, and you are successful. You move to London, pack your stuff into her car and drive to the apartment that you rent together because her boyfriend is doing her head in.

Being roommates is fun. You joke around about sharing a room like proper sisters. You steal each other's clothes. She teases you about your perfectly organised makeup in those clear plastic containers.

"You are such a robot," she says.

"No, just like things organised."

"It's definitely weird. No wonder Lisa dumped you."

"Okay, harsh."

"She did dump you though, it's a fact."

She smiles. It's banter.

"Okay, haha, I got dumped."

"Because you're a weirdo. Yeeaaaah, I just said that."

She walks off to her room, laughing.

You're going to need to develop that thick skin again.

*

You go for drinks to celebrate. She says she knows a good place to go. She has always had great taste like that. You notice a missing person poster on a street sign as you pass. You recognise May's punky hair.

"Oh my God, isn't that May?"

"Oh shit, yeah," she says. "Forgot to tell you about that. Yeah, May is missing."

"Holy shit, that's awful."

"Yeah, they reckon she's been kidnapped or something. I dunno. I mean, bad taste, but who the fuck would want to kidnap May?"

She laughs, and you forget about the poster.

*

The bar is old fashioned and cute, but unfortunately *full* of drunk people. You wait ages to get served. She invites some guys to come and sit with you. She tells them that she's your boss and laughs in your face when you deny it. The guys are about your age and are tight t-shirt wearing clones of each other. They laugh at her jokes and dominate any chance you get of having a quiet chat. You drink with them for a bit, then you get bored of them trying it on, showing off. You text her when you go to the loo asking to head somewhere else.

"Where do you have in mind?" She asks when you get back. "The lads know a good place around here."

She smiles because she knows what you were asking, really.

You go to the other pub with them. One of the guys grinds up against you while you wait for drinks at the bar. You tell him to fucking cut it out, and he laughs like you're playing. The four of you sit around a table, and you feel wrong in your outfit, that it's too short, too tight. He stares, and you hate her for putting you in this situation. You finish your drink and keep taking loo breaks to get away from his eyes on you. She laughs, showing off, telling them stories—embarrassing ones about you getting drunk and falling over.

"That's so hot," one of the guys says when she tells them about your ex-girlfriend.

"What is exactly?"

"You know, the whole girls kissing thing."

"Did you two ever . . . ?" The other one asks.

"Oh, *she* wishes," she says, shooting you a disdainful glance.

They laugh, and you feel too miserable and embarrassed to make a decent response. So, you roll your eyes and go outside for a smoke. You wish you could get the keys to the flat off her. You text her and ask for them, but she ignores you.

He follows you outside. You try to ignore him, but he keeps getting closer. He touches your hair, and you slap his hand away hard.

"Get the fuck away from me."

"She said you were up for it," he slurred, drunk and confused and disgusting.

"Yeah? Well, I'm not, so get the fuck away from me, okay?"

He leans in again, and you kick him hard in the shin and run back inside. You storm over to her and snatch her purse. She and the other guy are laughing. She tries to steal it back off you.

"Give me the key. I'm going home," you snap.

"Hey, come on, we're having fun."

"I'm not. You're the only one doing that. Give me the fucking key."

She yanks the handbag out of your hands.

"Calm down," she says.

"Fuck you!"

You feel embarrassed, and a bit sick and just want to leave.

"I want to go home!"

She laughs and tosses the keys at you; they clatter to the floor. She and the guy laugh as you scramble around in the dark, trying to find them. You turn off your phone as soon as you get back to the apartment, curl up in bed and try to calm down.

You feel sick, like you've made a colossal mistake. Is every day going to be like this?

You are so angry with her. You want to be surprised that she would do something as horrible as this. You're angry with yourself when you realise, you're not.

For the first time, you really want to hurt her. You're mad as hell. It's your way; you get scared, you get sad, and then you get mad. You find yourself in her room. You want to smash her mirror, take her favourite book, kick in her bed. You want to trash it, but it's already a mess. She's always been untidy. She said people with brains didn't have time for cleaning—usually whilst giving you a hard stare.

You go to rip one of her pictures from the wall. And you notice it's May's missing person poster. What the actual fuck? That's sick, even for her. You look at it properly now. There is May with her mohawk, smiling lazily at the camera. Missing since February 24th, last seen in Hyde Park.

Worse still, you notice that this picture isn't just mounted on the wall. It's framed. She's put it in a fucking ornate gold frame!

What the *fuck*.

You close the door and go back to your room. You feel freaked out in a way that you can't describe. You try to text one of your old friends about it but can't express the source of your discomfort. You sleep with your bedroom door locked.

*

The next day, she insists that she was just drunk and silly. She doesn't' say that she's sorry. She talks about what a creep that guy was and a total liar, saying that she'd given him a false impression about you. You tell yourself, that's probably true. She can be harsh at times, but she wouldn't do something like that. Besides, she's your friend, your sort-of sister. Of course you believe her over some creep.

You probably only got so upset because you were drunk.

Everything can be explained.

*

Things are typical for a while. Maybe not great-typical, but there's a routine.

Yes, she enjoys embarrassing you at work. That's annoying. Like when she sent you into a meeting with all the department heads without the briefing documents. Or when she had you order in all those pens from the dodgy supplier. Or that day she had you buy coffee for all the interviewees with your own credit card and wouldn't reimburse you. That sucked!

But at home, she's lovely. So fun! After that time with the coffee, she went and got you dried rose petals for your bath and ordered in from the charming Italian place up the road to say sorry. So sweet!

She tells you that she *has* to be a bitch at work because the team are really horrible, and you have to be kind of a dickhead to get ahead. She keeps telling you that it's nothing personal.

*

The flat is your space. You go to Ikea to get stuff for it. It sucks that the bathroom doesn't have a lock, but she spoke to the landlord, who said that he didn't want the flat to be modified at all. She actually really values your input when it comes to decorating. She's always gushing over your good taste.

You toast cheap prosecco to getting the decor just the way you wanted it, minus the bathroom lock.

Before this, you dreaded the thought of moving in together and having to lowkey live with a couple. But she tells you privately that her boyfriend is really getting on her nerves. You see it in action. One night, he comes over with Chinese for the three of you. She pushes him back into the hall and shuts the front door behind her. You hear her yelling at him, telling him how incredibly fucking presumptuous it is for him to come over just assuming on your dinner plans.

You feel bad for him as he carries the Chinese back to his car.

*

You see photos of May peering out at you on all the lamp posts on your walk to work. Her eyes seem to follow you around every street. The people in your office are nice, friendly even. The impression she created of them wasn't great, so you're relieved to find that this is not the case.

You notice that your co-workers don't seem to think much of her. They hide this well from you. You suspect it's the reason you don't get invited to come and bitch with them on coffee breaks after she sends everybody a memo.

One horrible Friday, she tosses her bag at you as you pack your things away.

"Carry that, wench," she says, laughing.

You can feel your face getting red as people stare.

"No way, carry it yourself."

She carries it home, and when you get back to work on Monday, she sends you a deadline that means you have to stay late. When you finally get home, you find she's been through your well organised makeup tray and removed a bunch of your lipsticks.

You are irritated. But you knew this might happen when you

took the job.

"Sorry, babes, I lost that red lipstick of yours," she tells you the next day over lunch. "No biggie, right?"

"You can always buy me a new one," you say.

Her expression stiffens. "Are you serious? You think they'd have even bothered looking at your application form without me?"

"So that gives you the right to go through my stuff, borrow things without asking, and then lose them?" You snap back.

She smirks then and starts to laugh. "What the fuck? I'm clearly joking. You used to be able to take a joke, oh my God! Of course, I'll replace it."

She never does, though.

*

After that first night, you are reluctant to go with her for a drink. You don't want to be a part of her weird vanity project while she's on/off with her boyfriend. It always ends the same way when you do. Men come over and try their luck in bars. She lets them sit with you both. She laughs at their jokes. She undermines you. She allows them to feel her up under the table. She got a man to pay for your taxi once, let him walk to your door.

"We're a couple," she tells him when he tries to kiss her. "You have the wrong idea."

"A couple?" He repeats. "Bullshit. You said you were sisters before."

You are stuck behind them in the stairwell as she plays with the keys. Why the fuck won't she just ask the landlord for another set of keys?

"Look, this was super fun, but yeah, I'm not interested. Go home."

She laughs in his face when he tries to argue.

"You had your hand on my—"

"Look, go home," you tell him. "You're tired of this. You're tired of her. "Seriously, just fuck off."

He shoves you hard out of the way, sending you to the ground. Your favourite pair of shoes—spiky black stilettos—snap, and she starts laughing hysterically. She falls against the front door she's laughing so hard.

"Oh my God! What an idiot! What an actual idiot!"

She keeps laughing as she opens the door, then sways drunkenly into her bedroom. Your shoulder hurts, and you lock your door again when you get to your room.

You can't sleep. You wonder if she's looking at that framed poster of May, *missing* May, in her room. So fucked up. You find yourself wondering about Claudia, who kissed you back when you were too shy to even admit you liked girls. You wonder if Claudia knows about May. You know that she used to go and visit her in uni. There are photos of the three of them all hanging out together. The posters are everywhere, but from Instagram—the only social media Claudia seems to use—you can see that Claudia is wandering around Thailand.

Hi Claudia, long time no see.

You close the message and start again.

Hi Claudia. I hope everything's good. Photos look amazing (!!!!). I don't know if you're aware, but I just thought you should know. May Connelly is missing. She's been gone since February, according to the police. There are posters everywhere. I'm really sorry if you had to find out this way.

You hit send.

She might be asleep. You don't know much about time differences. You unlock your door and head out into the kitchen to get a glass of water. Her phone has been left on the countertop, and the contents of her handbag spilt out over the floor. As you reach for an empty glass, her phone flashes on. You see your own name on the screen. Your blood runs cold as you re-read the message you've just sent to Claudia's account.

A nasty thought flashes through your head. You try and remember if Claudia had an Instagram account before or after she went off travelling.

Then you look up and see her staring at you with bloodshot eyes.

"What are you doing?"

Her tone is friendly, but her face is completely blank.

"Getting water."

"Getting water," she repeats, wrinkling her nose. "Why were you looking at my phone?"

"I wasn't."

"I wasn't," she snears after you again.

"Why are you getting notifications for Claudia Shephard's Instagram? I just messaged her."

She laughs. "Thinking about her up late at night, were you? Oh my God, you're such a creeper." She laughs again, shaking her head. "Miss Holier-Than-Thou-I've-Got-The-Travel-Bug-Claudia? Pfft. The idiot hasn't changed her password in like four years. She's all look at my wanderlust on fucking Instagram, but her messages are all lonely and needy. People can be so fake!"

"Are you serious?"

"Oh, fuck off." She laughs and slides her phone back into her pocket. "Come on, when did you get so boring?"

It's something else she does. If she disagrees, she is so quick to climb up onto the high ground and sneer down at you in shocked dismay. But if it's the other way around, she laughs and fixes you with a long stare, acts as if you're a kid or too dumb to understand the joke.

"It's not boring to think you should respect other people's privacy."

"Oh, boo-hoo, what are you? Her girlfriend or something? You wish." She pulls back her hair and smirks at you. "When a guy behaves this way, we don't hesitate to call him out on being gross. Think about that, Little Lou."

She struts off to her room, and you hear her laughing to herself.

*

You get promoted, move to a new department, away from your sort-of sister. You go for drinks with people from the office. She is never invited. You don't make it obvious, but you start ignoring her texts.

In retaliation, she starts inviting her boyfriend round more. They treat the flat like it's their space and you are slowly but surely driven back into your room. There is laundry on every seat of the sofa, on the armrests, even on the kitchen countertops. Never-ending fucking laundry. He is always cooking but never washes up. You're so over the whole student passive-aggressive flatmate horseshit.

You keep your kitchen things in your room and use them as you go. You see her boyfriend naked more than you ever imagined you would.

They joke around when they see you, act totally surprised that you still live there. You spend more time at work; you chat with people around the office. You don't object when the four girls you've become friendly with subtly bitch about her. You don't care anymore. It's not like she's even your real sister. Your parents married when both of you were in your twenties. You don't have to be loyal in the way that she insists family always is.

You go out for beers and come back to the sound of bedsprings, hushed whispering, and intimate moans.

You sleep with headphones and start saving to live somewhere else.

*

One Friday night, you discover to your delight that you're getting the place all to yourself. The two of them have managed to dress themselves *and* leave the flat somehow. She leaves lipstick stains on the bathroom mirror and nail varnish dashes on the door like paint.

You tell yourself that you are *not* going to clean any of it.

Instead, you order a pizza and veg out in front of the television with some wine. It's fun for a while. You finish your food and get comfy lying across the seats.

But that is when you notice it.

Something is digging into your lower back. You wriggle around, shift your position, but the middle cushion is so stiff. You pull it out to flip it over, but the bottom is discoloured, there's even a hole. The sofa is hers from her old place, and you figure she'd throw a hissy fit about you changing it. So, you push your hands along the front, and as you do, the more it seems like there's something lodged in there. You unzip the side and push your hand through, and sure enough, there's a plastic bag.

You pull it out, unfold it, and inside, you can see a mobile phone and what appears to be a slim silver necklace. You open the bag, and on further inspection, discover the necklace is a tiny crescent moon. You raise it to your face and see blood speckled along its surface.

'Hippy garbage, who would wear that?'

Her words flash through your head, and suddenly you remember seeing this necklace peering out at you from around May's neck on every missing person poster in the city. Your first instinct is to bundle the necklace back into the bag, stuff it in the sofa and never mention it again. You drop it from your hand, and it clatters onto the coffee table. You remember reading in the paper that May's mobile phone was never found. There is blood on the cracked screen.

You fix up the sofa and take the phone and the necklace back to your room. You try to calm down, but it doesn't work, and you vomit up your pizza and your wine. You sit there panicking, trying to imagine your next move.

Do you confront her? Or just call the police?

She comes back before you make up your mind. You lock your door and hear her head in without her boyfriend, singing at the top of her voice. She's drunk. You can hear from the rustle of plastic that she has brought food back with her.

You dial 999 on your phone but don't manage to actually call.

You try and tell yourself that there could be several reasons for her to have May's phone, and you know . . . there are. But none of them are good.

"You up?" she calls through your door.

You sit there in silence, drumming your fingers against the cotton of your pyjamas. You try and breathe slowly, like a normal person. Where the hell did she get May's phone? How did she get it?

"Helloooooooo!" she calls again, rapping her fingers against the door now. "Your light is on. Come on, don't ignore me. Little Loooou!"

You shiver. Creepy. She's so fucking creepy. And you never saw any of that, did you?

Lisa always called her creepy. But you didn't think that. You liked her—your sort-of sister, who was so much cooler than you. You were jealous of her punk-rock princess silver hair, her shawls and her combat boots. You wanted to be funnier, wittier, more like her.

You were so busy being distracted by all that, that you never realised she was *really* creepy.

"Come on, don't be mad at me," she called. "Sulking is soooo dumb."

You hide May's things in your pillowcase and open the door, squinting and rubbing your eyes. "What?"

"Oh wow, did you fall asleep with the light on? How responsible of you," she says, chuckling to herself as she pushed past you to climb onto your bed. You try to hide your horror as she props up your pillows to lean back against them.

"You do realise that you're choosing to ignore the word 'asleep' there, right?"

"Wow, not very friendly," she says, shaking her head. "I just wanted to let you know that I've had a think about what you said, and I've logged out of Claudia's Instagram permanently. I was being shitty before. I'm sorry."

She offers you her hand to shake, so you take it and decide that it would be very easy for her to close down an Instagram that she set up in the first place.

"I made you some tea. Here."

She's never made you tea before. You take it and wonder if it's paranoid of you to think she's poisoned it. She snuggles back against the pillowcase, and you can feel your heartbeat in your ears as you watch to see if she can feel the phone against her back. You sit at the corner of the bed

"Thanks for that."

"I hate that we haven't been getting along, you know. Robbie and I have kind of taken over the flat, and I barely see you now you've moved departments."

"I know. So weird, right?"

"I have lost a lot of friends in the past because we grew apart. I'd really hate for that to happen to us."

"Just stay on my sweet side, okay?"

She smiles and stretches.

"Uncomfortable pillow," she says.

You shrug and sip your tea. She yells "PILLOW FIGHT," and suddenly the phone hardened pillow strikes you across the face with a thunk. The telephone and necklace slide out, you drop your tea, and the handle smashes on the ground, the contents soaking into the carpet.

The two of you sit there frozen.

Then she stands and picks up the bag.

"Oh," she says, breaking the silence. "Where did Little Lou find this little thing?"

"The sofa."

Her expression is blank. "Oh yeah, I figured it'd be safe in there."

"Why do you have that stuff?"

"What do you mean?" She stares at you with those horrible void eyes.

"That's May's, right?"

She smiles, and somehow that is worse.

"May had a lot of really great qualities, you know? So confident, a great debater, and, seriously, so *confident*. She rocked the whole half-shaved head thing. Great taste in clothes."

"But," she continues, "She had a lot of really wasteful stuff going on as well. Like the whole hipster bullshit with technology? Look at this piece of junk. It survived getting hit by my car, and there's only the slightest scratch on it."

You think about getting up, shoving her drunk ass out of the way. But somehow, you're still sat there.

"Nothing to say? Figured if you felt bold enough to snoop through my sofa like a maniac, you might have something to add."

Your voice trembles, and you hate yourself for it.

"So-so you're saying you killed her? Is that seriously what you're saying?"

She rolls her eyes. "Oh my God. Obviously." She shoves the bag of evidence into her back pocket and folds her arms. "I asked her to meet me for a chat, hit her with my car, brought her back to Robbie's old apartment, chopped her into little pieces, and ate her in a stew."

You feel every hair stand up on the back of your neck.

"Are you fucking serious?"

She starts to laugh. It's a sound you're so used to, but now it makes you feel sick.

"I like to be around people who make me look better. People who bring out the best in me, who make me the best possible version of myself."

You get up and go to push past her, but she grabs your wrist, her hand clamps down on your thigh, and she forces you back into a seated position on your bed.

"No, no, I want to chat." She smiles, then wrinkles her nose in disgust. "Ew, are you sweating? Gross."

"I don't want to talk."

Her face creases up in amusement.

"You know, you don't look so good. I think you should take that trip you've been talking about. Hell, maybe you could meet up with Claudia along the way."

"Get off me!" The panic in your voice horrifies you and

delights her.

You manage to wrestle free and shove her as hard as you can. You reach the door when she smashes into you from behind. Your chin slams into the floor, and your head spins. She sits down on your lower back, and the air is crushed out of you.

"Why?" you gasp out.

She laughs and sighs, wriggling her hips, making herself comfortable. "I remember reading about these tribes who would eat parts of their enemy to gain their powers. It's super gross, but interesting, right? So I applied that knowledge to Grace, who was my buddy in primary school. We were eleven. I ate her hands and learned to draw."

You've seen her sketches in charcoal, her beautiful art on the walls.

"You're full of shit!"

"No, seriously, Grace Matthews, age eleven, goes missing on school trip to France. Body is found disturbingly without hands four years later. I got a teacher fired over that; we were left unsupervised a *lot*. Grace fell and hit her head when we went exploring in a cave. She was alive when I took her hands. I guess it was shock and blood loss that killed her really. Never mind. I was young and freaked out, so I held off doing it again for a while. Stay still. Come on. Now Sabrina got on my nerves. She was so boring and too pretty to even realise that she was fucking putting everyone around her to sleep. So beautiful without any substance."

She laughs and pushes your face into the floor. "Claudia could own a room with just a couple of phrases. Made me witty, made me flirty. I got so much better at all that. And come on, you liked the little travel blog I set up in her memory, didn't you? You even believed it was her reading your sad fucking messages, Little Lou. And May, well, I covered her already. You know, I think they'd all be happy for me." She smashes your head into the floor, harder now. You struggle and feel her nails dig into the sides of your face.

You start wriggling under her, thrashing about, jerking your torso up into her, twisting your head. She loses her grip, and you crawl to your feet, frantic. You let out a hysterical screech and wave your arm blindly behind you to try and push her back. You race to the bathroom door and slam it shut. You press your whole body against it, both hands holding the door handle up. The landlord wouldn't let you install a lock—like fuck, she probably didn't even ask.

"Things have been getting dull between us, you know?" she calls. "You skulking around with the office bimbos, ignoring my texts. We're meant to be family. We live under the same roof, and you barely give me the time of day anymore."

She taps on the door.

"You can't even tell when I'm joking anymore?"

"You're fucking sick!"

You feel the tears brim in your eyes and spill down your cheeks. You keep your feet tight to the door.

"Just fuck off! JUST GET AWAY!"

She laughs and kicks the door hard. You hear her footsteps drift off into the flat. You shove the sanitary bin against the door and search the bathroom cabinet frantically for something you can use to defend yourself.

You find a pair of blunted nail scissors that are probably more suited for an infant's nails than the skin of an adult. Still, you hold them tight in your hand and press yourself against the door, heart pounding in your ears, listening and waiting.

Nail scissors? Seriously? Those ones? Oh my God. You'd have better luck trying to hit me in the head with one of those bloated bottles of conditioner.

You're freaking out now.

"How do you know what I'm—"

Oh, come off it. I know you. And you think you know me, but you don't. I know what you're going to do, how you put things together, how you act. I even know that in a minute, you'll make a break for it. Open that door, dash for the exit, try and stab me with those cute little scissors when I go to stop you.

Let me save you the trouble. It won't work, Little Lou. And

trying to overpower me won't work either. Sabrina took judo from age twelve to sixteen. And you know, since I ate her brain—I had it on pizza, in case you're wondering—I've gotten really good at disarming people and knocking them down.

Oh, there you go with the waterworks. You cry so easily. That's always been a trait I admired about you. It makes people trust you.

Why don't you just come out?

Come on.

Come outside, Little Lou.

You really don't want me to come in there after you. Trust me.

You scream and make a run for the door anyway. Those blunt baby scissors don't even pierce the skin of my hand. I grab your arm and twist it up. The scissors end up on the floor, and so do you. You start squirming like a pig in a net.

Luckily, I went and got the big knife. Don't cry. I'm being so nice to you compared to how I was with the others. May was always very compassionate. She's been a good influence on me.

Just like you.

THERE'S SOMETHING WRONG WITH ROSA

My sister's phone rings. It goes on for a few minutes, then a male voice answers.

"Hello, Rosa's phone."

"John, I want to talk to Rosa. Is she there?"

"Laura, how nice to hear from you. No, I'm afraid she's resting at the moment."

"I'm coming over to the clinic tomorrow. I want to see how she's doing."

"There's really no need. She's still undergoing treatment. I'd hate for you to waste a trip for her to sleep through your visit."

"It's no trouble at all. Expect me there tomorrow afternoon."

"Well, alright, but again, I'll update you if her condition improves."

"I'll be able to see that for myself tomorrow. Goodbye."

Three weeks he has derailed any contact I've attempted to have with my sister. My apparently hospitalised sister. Three weeks of being dodged and condescended to. Three weeks of her husband informing us all that there's something wrong with Rosa.

*

I have never liked my sister's husband. I didn't like him when he was Rosa's friend, I really didn't like him when they started dating, and I prayed to God that some divine act would disrupt the wedding.

To this day, I can't put my finger on the source of my dislike. Over the years, I've suspected it to be several things. If I was to try and describe it, I'd say . . . Okay, okay, okay, you know that feeling you get when you see something disgusting? Like, someone vomiting, picking their nose, or rubbing the front of their trousers in public? Something inside you recoils in disgust. It's something you see before you that you just know is wrong. It's kind of like that.

When we first met, he was seventeen. He couldn't stand without leaning on whatever surface was nearest: a countertop, a chair, my car, a very fragile cabinet etc. He squinted when he spoke as if carrying on a sentence was extremely hard for him. He felt the need to use your name whenever he spoke directly to you. His laugh was a bark. He would leave the toilet seat up when he went for a piss, leaving drops of urine to drip down onto the cream carpet, marking his territory. Rosa would mention it to him, and he would feign ignorance but carry on doing it. He would always compare himself to her, always insisting that he was more intelligent, better liked, funnier and better qualified than Rosa. How lucky she was to have snared a guy like him. But at seventeen, he was merely obnoxious.

My parents just *loved* him, still just *love* him, in that way that parents always inconveniently do. To this day, nobody else knows what I'm talking about. The leaning, the barking, the pissing, none of that got to anyone else. Not even Rosa seemed to mind the way he condescended her.

At seventeen, she said, "You're oversensitive. This is why I have a boyfriend, and you don't."

"If having a boyfriend means smiling like an idiot while getting insulted, then I'm fine as I am."

"He's not insulting me, he's playing around."

Yes, that was how she put it. He was playful and fun; I just couldn't take a joke. Then again, Rosa never had an excellent track record with listening to me.

We are six years apart, so our relationship was built on me bossing Rosa around and her rebelling. I remember a time when she was so small I could pick her up and carry her everywhere. With everything that happened, I find myself thinking about that now.

When did you get so big, Rosa?

*

As the youngest of four, Rosa was spoilt by everyone except me. Our mother used to say that I was born forty-five, I transitioned from sulking child to sulking adult. As my little playmate, Rosa would sit with me while we played 'board meeting.' She would be sat on my lap and end up falling asleep as I tried to educate her on dinosaurs or the water cycle.

People have always tended to describe Rosa as 'the pretty one.' Both myself and my older sister have our dad's thick eyebrows and square jaw. Dad used to joke that I looked exactly like him in a long black wig. It's not the most flattering description. Rosa and our brother look like our Mum, with eyes like almonds, glossy hair, long limbs, and smooth skin.

Mum used to worry that her looks would make her shallow. With Maritza dating girls and my lack of interest in anything non-marketable, there was only Rosa to worry about when it came to boys.

"I don't want her to be like my sister," Mum would say disapprovingly.

"Aunt Maria is married," Benito said. "She has three kids, all with the same guy."

"She has grown up, but when we were young, she flitted from one boy to the next. It was embarrassing. I don't want Rosa to grow up to be some flashy woman."

Mum's worries were senseless; Rosa had no idea how to flirt. Once, she asked me how it was done, and as I had no clue either, the discussion was brief. Unlike our Aunt Maria, teenage Rosa was all about her friends. She hung around a group of frivolous girls, who would come over to the house and shriek whenever Benito was in the room. Guys would ask her out, but she didn't care about any of that stuff. Any interested parties were always turned down politely with an offer of friendship instead.

"Men in real life are so unromantic," she declared. She was lying flat on the sofa, scrolling through her phone. The screen came up from over my head, displaying a picture of a smirking, shirtless teenage boy. "Why would anyone think I'd want to see that?"

"Preview of the goods?"

"Seriously?" she gasped, laughing.

"God, no, I'm kidding. Get that thing away from me," I said, batting her away.

"So gross," she said. "How is the human race going to go on if guys act like that?"

I sometimes wonder if Rosa hadn't been clueless at flirting, would she have ended up with that creep, John? Would she be married to someone like Uncle Janos, someone quiet and dependable, once all the exciting, dangerous men had been seen to?

John was her first boyfriend. They met in school, and when they started sixth form, he asked her out officially. By this time, I was finishing my first degree, and she called me up for a chat. Even now, well into her thirties, Rosa only calls when there's something dramatic or important to discuss. Generally, she texts to a religious degree.

"So, listen, I have some news."

"Good news?"

"I think so," she said nervously. "I kind of have a boyfriend." There was a nervous pause. "You remember my friend, John?"

"The John who squinted and sat on the bumper of my car?" I said. "Oh."

"Hey, don't be like that," she protested. "He's a great guy. You'd actually really like him."

"Okay, Okay. If you say so."

"You spoil everything, Laura! You're so judgmental all the time!"

She reacted this way every time anyone said anything critical of him. She still does.

*

She started acting strangely over a month ago.

"Hello?"

"Laura, it's me."

"Hey, how are you?"

"I don't know. I'm not sure."

"What?"

"When we were kids, you found it so hard to sleep. Mum used to say that your brain was too busy for you to rest. Do you remember that, Laura?"

Her tone was far away, distant like she was sleep talking.

"Yeah, I guess," I said, frowning and twisting away from my desk. "Are you having trouble sleeping?"

"How did you manage to sleep when we were little?"

"I'd just get tired enough, kind of drift off. It was just—I'd tucker myself out."

"And that was it?"

"Yeah, I don't really remember. Hey, is everything okay?"

Rosa started crying weakly.

"Rosa? What's the matter? Do you want me to come over?"

The crying drew to an abrupt halt.

"No."

"You're kind of scaring me," I said.

She laughed at that. "Nothing scares you."

"You can see why I'm concerned. What's the matter with you?"

"I'm just having trouble sleeping. It's been . . . playing with my head."

I sighed, rubbing my temples. When we were kids, Rosa would cry and act up if she didn't get her full eight hours. "Maybe cut back on your time at the store for a bit. You need to take care of yourself."

"You're right. You're absolutely right."

"Rosa, are you sure you don't want me to drive down? If I leave at five, I can make it there by eight."

"No, no, I'm just being stupid. You're busy, and I'm being selfish."

"We're sisters, who else can we be selfish with?"

She laughed again.

"I'm going to try and rest my eyes. I love you."

"I love you too."

The next and last time we spoke was two weeks after that. She answered her phone, exhausted and barely coherent.

"I'm sorry, I'm too tired. Here, talk to John."

He has been answering her phone ever since.

*

"So, Laura, Rosa tells me you're graduating soon. Any plans for work?"

"I'm starting an MBA in September," I said. "What about you? Any lofty university aspirations after your A-Levels?"

Rosa glared at me across the table.

He squeezed her arm gently and smiled. "Yes, actually, Laura, I'm going to study medicine at the University of York."

"We've never had a doctor in the family before," our Mum said appreciatively.

"Mum! You're embarrassing me!" Rosa protested.

The first dinner with John made three courses seem like thirty. He would address each of us by name like he was answering to a panel. I drove Martiza home as we couldn't all fit into Dad's car.

"What do you think of that guy?" I asked, wrinkling my nose.

"He seems nice," she said. "Rosa looks happy."

"I thought he was a jackass."

"Oh, come on."

"Oh, come on, yourself! 'In answer to your question, Martiza', 'Well, Martiza', 'And that's what I think about that, Martiza.'"

"He's just polite."

"It wasn't polite; it was vaguely violating."

She laughed. "As if you were ever going to like Little Rosa's first love."

"First love? Please, he's some boy she's dating."

"You're such a romantic."

*

Five years ago, that loser was interviewed by a women's fashion magazine. You know, the kind of trash that tells you you're getting your orgasms wrong, or about the new celebrity diet you're not crazy enough to try, or flashes you twenty pages of clothes that the insipid teenage girls who buy into all of that could never afford. They interviewed him because he had earned a good reputation as a plastic surgeon. The kind of twisted world we are living in where a man is praised for his ability to reshape women's bodies to his own ditzy whims, you tell me.

They asked if he would ever perform surgery for a loved one. John had (brackets) laughed and said that there was no need, as his wife Rosa was the most beautiful woman in the world.

Rosa showed me the article—how charming it was for him to say something like that.

"Some doctor. And he has the gall to brag about it." I said, wrinkling my nose in disgust. "He's a plastic surgeon. What is he contributing to society?"

"Better noses," Rosa said, smirking.

*

At Benito's birthday party four years ago, John moved from irritating to something that worried me considerably.

Benito had booked a hotel reception with a fancy garden (at the end of the evening, he would reveal his engagement to his long-suffering girlfriend, hence the efforts with the venue).

I had arrived early to help prepare, Rosa was supposed to join me, but she texted to say that she was running late. The venue was all set up, and the guests started to arrive. Benito was in full hosting mode, Martiza was setting up the music. I texted Rosa to ask if she had set off. No reply.

I reluctantly texted John to ask if he had spoken to Rosa.

We are on our way now. Rosa's phone died.

Irritating.

The party was in full swing when they got there. I was chatting to a colleague of my brother's when I noticed Rosa on the dance floor. She hadn't said she'd arrived. Maybe she hadn't been there long? Only the way she swayed and stumbled . . . she seemed drunk.

My sister has never had much of a head for alcohol. She tried one of Dad's beers once when she was nine and subsequently pretended to be sick for the next twenty minutes until Dad told her to grow up.

I went over and tapped her arm.

Rosa turned towards me, brown eyes wide and unfocused.

"What's wrong with you?"

She wrapped her arms around my shoulders and tried to pull me in to dance with her. Her breath stank of wine, and she laughed, head tossed back. I wriggled out of her grip, and she stumbled into my arms.

"Rosa?"

"I feel funny," she said.

"Come on, let's get you some water."

"I want to dance," she said, swaying as she stood still. "Let me dance a little longer. You're all strict like John."

"I'm way worse than John. Come on." I took her arm, and she reluctantly followed me. I sat her down on a table by the window and handed her a glass of water. Away from the strobe lights, she looked pale, sweating and confused.

Her head drooped, and she stared down at her trembling knees.

"What's the matter with you?"

"I don't know. Now I feel kind of stupid."

I smiled and sat back, touching her forehead. She was burning up. "You feel hot. Do you have a fever?"

"A bit. John said that might happen."

"You silly girl. You shouldn't have come if you weren't well. Beni wouldn't have minded." I took her hands and squeezed them gently.

Tears trickled down her cheeks and dropped onto our linked hands.

"I don't feel well," she mumbled.

"Let me get you some water. Wait right here."

I returned with water to find Rosa gone. I spotted her and John at the entrance, his arm around her shoulder. Her head slumped down like a child in trouble. I called after her, but my shout was lost over the music.

*

I thought she would leave him once. Seven years ago, so they had been married for just one year. They were fighting a lot. She never told me what about. She told me that she felt overwhelmed, consumed, like she couldn't think or breathe without him. So she packed a bag and called me to say she was coming to stay for a while. I set up the guest room, I'd offered to come and get her, but she wanted to talk to him before she left.

She said she found him holding her dress like a baby, weeping into it like every second she was gone would last a thousand years for him. It was intense for him too; she wasn't alone feeling like that. So, she couldn't leave him.

My guest room stayed ready for a year, just in case.

Once they came over for coffee, I found him in the corridor on his way back from the bathroom, staring in at the room that would have been hers if she'd left that night.

He smiled at me and said nothing.

*

Out of the blue, six months ago, that stupid man stopped being a plastic surgeon. Even I could admit that it was at the height of his success. But off he went and opened his own medical practice out in the countryside. It was an hour's drive from Rosa's shop in the city. She had started selling antiques and other overpriced pretty accessories.

I suggested that she get her own apartment in the city and commute to see him on weekends. Of course, she wouldn't hear of it. What do I know? I'm only her sister.

It meant we saw less of her.

Sometimes she would call before she closed up her shop, always cheerful, though often a little drained. I would nag her, and she would laugh.

They live in a big house in the country, walking distance from his medical practice. The town smelled like animal faeces and appeared to be populated by fresh-faced Little House on the Prairie types. Rosa is referred to as 'The doctor's *Spanish* (they whisper the word *Spanish*) wife.' The people are friendly but tend to speak very-very slowly when addressing Rosa or any of us when we visit.

She finds it funny. I try hard to stop my eyes from rolling all the way back into my skull.

The last time I visited, complete strangers kept asking me if I was struggling to adjust to the weather around here. Before I could respond, Rosa started laughing and wrapped a scarf around my neck.

"Silly, you forgot your scarf!"

I hate visiting, but I do.

*

I don't doubt that he loves her. For the longest time, that was why I tolerated him when I realised that her mind would not be changed. It was clear he adored her. Despite his stupid self-promoting chatter, despite all that nonsense, it was clear that love was there. So although I hoped that she might find someone better or just leave him behind, I decided that if he loved her, that would have to be enough.

As long as she was safe.

*

The first time he removed her from us was two years ago. Martiza called my personal phone while I was in a meeting. She told me that she tried to call Rosa and John said to her that Rosa was in the hospital. She didn't sound concerned; John assured her that she was only there as a precaution. She told me that I was being crazy and to go have a baby so Rosa could retire from her position as my child.

I resisted swearing at her so I could ask which hospital she was in. Of course, it was no hospital at all—just his poxy little surgery in the boonies. My car got filthy from the country roads, and once I arrived, I made the elderly receptionist cry when she tried to explain to me in very slow English that the Doctor was unavailable at the moment.

Her sobs drew John from an office where he tried to greet me with a hug. I pushed him back and demanded to see my sister at once.

"Rosa really isn't well. I'm sure she wouldn't want you to see her in the state she's in."

"You keep saying she's ill, never anything specific! Just ill! Well, she's in this made-up version of a hospital, so you tell me now what's actually wrong with her," I yelled, jabbing his chest with my finger.

He dusted down his lab coat and stepped back, still smiling. Always smiling.

"Laura, I understand you're upset, but please calm down. Rosa is really unwell. She's resting. You can come when she feels better. She would be embarrassed for you to see her like this."

"I have known her every day of her life!" I closed the gap

between us. "So, you take me to her, or I'm calling the police."

His smile didn't fade.

"Fine. Come along, but she won't thank you for it."

'Come along,' like he was giving me permission to see my own sister.

*

No answer again. At least before he was answering her phone. Now he ignores the calls. My texts go unreturned.

I check my mobile again. This is distracting me. I just want to know that she is alright. I can't talk to the others. They trust John knows best. They trust him with Rosa. They think he treats her like she's made of glass, like something precious. They take it at face value. They *trust* him.

I spend my lunch break trying to get connected to no avail.

*

He told me that Rosa had been depressed. I told him that it was rubbish, that she wasn't the type. He shook his head and, avoiding my gaze, said that Rosa miscarried a baby, that she had become hysterical, unable to face the world. She had to be sedated after becoming violent.

There was a bruise on his wrist—I noticed it as he prepared the coffee. She had always wanted to be a mother. She imagined the names of her children before she was even in school. I would love a niece or nephew, even if it was fathered by that man.

He showed me to her, and her face broke my heart.

She was pale and withdrawn, sat up against the pillows. Her eyes open, but she didn't seem aware of us when we came in. John kissed the top of her head as he rearranged her pillows.

I held her hands and told her that I was so sorry.

A month later, she came to visit our parents, and we all acted like it never happened. When the two of us were alone, I waited and waited for her to mention it, but she never did. It just hung between us. I wondered if it was the same for her and that awful man, as I never heard of them trying again.

It was too painful for us all to talk about. For a while, when things were quiet, I'd notice this sad look on her face. Like she was thinking about something that I just couldn't comprehend.

*

"John, I want to see my sister."

"She really isn't in the condition to see anyone," he said.

"If she is depressed, she should be with her family. She should be with me."

He sighed. "No, Laura. She must remain at my clinic. I'm sorry, but I'd rather not worry you with the details. She is getting the care she needs. I know what is best for my wife."

I recheck my bag before I leave the office. I make sure to let my secretary know where I'm going. Just in case. Who knows what that man is capable of?

I don't bother calling her before I start my car. I know she isn't in a situation where the two of us can talk at the moment.

*

When Rosa was little, she used to draw her dream husband all the time. She'd use my Etch A Sketch and get really embarrassed if I asked to see. Of course, I managed to sneak a peek a few times. She always drew a wobbly looking Prince Charming, like something out of a Disney movie.

I guess it's a lot of little girls' dreams to marry Prince Charming.

Last summer we were all at a barbecue at my parent's house. Martiza couldn't come, neither could Beni. So, I was alone with my folks and Rosa and John. This meant Mum kept finding odd ways to ask when I was going to get married.

"Don't you want to be with your Prince Charming, just like Little Rosa?" She said, nudging John playfully.

John straight away started defending me in the way he knows I hate. "Oh, Laura is her own Prince Charming, I'm sure."

Mum and Dad laughed along, I frowned and said something scathing, but I noticed the look on Rosa's face. It was like she was going to be sick.

When I asked her about it later as the two of us did the dishes, she feigned ignorance. I asked her—I remember asking her, "Is everything alright with you two?"

And she gave me this *look*. I feel disturbed just thinking about it. This unnatural smile, these vacant eyes that did not belong to the sister I knew. She said, "Of course. We couldn't be happier." I felt my skin crawl like I'd suddenly been pushed into icy water.

Her whole marriage has been like that for me.

*

This time I arrived just before visiting hours ended. I wouldn't be told no by his flimsy and incompetent staff again. "I am here to see Rosa Kildare. I'm her sister. Can you let me know which room she is in?"

The girl on reception frowned, pooling through her records.

"I'm very sorry, but Mrs Kildare is not currently a patient with us. She's resting at home. Doctor Kildare has been away from the office for a few days to take care of her."

Have you ever had one of those moments where it's like all the blood in your body just drains out of you? In the clinic, he said. He told me that Rosa was in the clinic and couldn't be moved from there—that she needed care. He was *lying!* I knew it! I knew he was lying.

I heard the receptionist calling after me as I flew out of the room. The clinic door slammed behind me. My feet pounded on the pavement as I ran back to my car. I could hear my heart in my chest slamming against my ribs. I turned the ignition. I knew the way to their house from here. It wasn't far. I knew I was right about that disgusting little liar. I was so sure! I never should have let things get this far.

What the hell was he doing to my sister?

The house was quiet, secluded from the rest of the village. It circled back onto the woods. There was a large front garden that Rosa had taken particular pride in. She always had a way of taking something simple and making it beautiful. It's how she could turn grubby relics from dull lives into beautiful antiques, how she could make any meal look as though it had been crafted by a professional chef.

If I had seen the house sooner, I would have known there was a problem. The garden, in which my sister had spent so much of her time and energy, was in a state of decay. Flowers crippled and wilted in their beds, hedges overgrown and laden with thorns. Leaves littered the ground like rubbish. His car wasn't there, I realised with relief.

I parked closer to the woods so he wouldn't see my car if he came home. Rushing to the front door, I started banging, shouting her name. In the background, I could faintly see someone through the thick decorative glass.

"Rosa! Rosa, let me in! It's Laura!"

When no response came, I bent down, opening the letterbox. I saw a woman with long black hair dash out of sight.

"Rosa, it's Laura. I'm getting you out of here! Stand back, I'm going to smash a window."

I could hear terrified whispering.

I found a rock in the flowerbed and smashed the window by the front door handle. Relieved for their lack of neighbours, I flinched at the sound. I could hear a woman's voice now, hushed and frantic.

"Rosa!"

Careful not to catch my skin on the jagged, broken glass, I managed to open the front door. My shoes crunched on the shards as I stepped inside.

"Rosa, it's me, come on!"

The smell hit me instantly. Usually, my sister's home smelled like flowery candles, scents she would sell at her shop. Now there was a kind of sickly clinical smell in the air, like hand sanitiser or an anti-bacterial spray. I crept through the living room.

"Rosa, it's Laura . . ."

Rosa was huddled up on the floor. Her hands over her head. She had tried to conceal herself behind the curtains. She was whimpering and crying like a small child. She was wearing a hospital gown—did that idiot think he could make his house into some kind of hospital that she wasn't allowed to leave? And I could see bandages on her neck, on her forehead, concealed by her fringe.

"Rosa? It's me. Everything is alright now."

I reached out and touched her arm gently. Rosa flinched like I'd burned her. She pulled her hands away from her head and stared up at me with a terrified expression I didn't recognise. No, it was like she didn't recognise me.

"Please don't hurt me! Please don't! Don't!"

That woman who wore my sister's face, she spoke in another voice. Her accent was thick, like someone from the Midlands, and she sounded . . . young. She sounded like a teenager, high pitched and frantic.

"What?" I stepped back from her. That feeling again, like all the blood had dropped from my body. Hot bile rising in my throat, I clutched at my chest. "You're not Rosa—"

"NO! NO! I AM! I AM! I AM!" The teenage girl who wore my sister's face screamed. "I'm Rosa!"

I staggered back, and she dove forwards, wrapping her bandaged arms around my leg, screaming at me. I stumbled against the wall, trying to prise myself free.

"I'm Rosa! I'm Rosa! I'm Rosa Kildare! I'm twenty-nine, my husband is a doctor! I run a shop, I sell antiques! My favourite colour is bronze!" She screamed and clawed at me, trying to use me to pull herself upright. "Please! Please!"

"Let go of me!"

I pushed at her face. Her skin felt hard and stiff, almost like she'd had . . . almost like she'd had surgery. Her eyes were wide and frantic, boring into mine. Saliva spilt from her mouth, down her chin and onto my skirt. I recoiled in disgust, trying to push her away; it was like she couldn't close her mouth properly.

"Where is my sister!" I cried, "Where is Rosa!"

"NO! NO!"

She managed to knock me down onto my back. I tried to push her off as she climbed on top of me, pulling my hair, shaking me.

"You don't understand! I'm Rosa. He'll kill me if—"

"Rosa," John called from the living room. "What on earth are you doing?"

He stood in the living room doorway, watching us with the kind of flat, cold expression I had seen whenever he didn't know I was looking. It was the face he didn't like to show off.

"John," the teenager wailed. "John!" She seemed inconsolable as she climbed off me. She rushed to him, stumbling on her shaking, bandaged legs. He pulled her close to him, stroking her hair.

"It's alright," he said. "This is your sister, Laura. Did you forget?"

"I'm sorry," she cried. "I'm sorry."

"To be fair to you, Laura should have knocked on the front door like a proper guest. Oh, you must have been frightened." He glanced down at the broken glass beneath his feet before running his hands through her long dark hair. "Are you hurt?"

She shook her head, wiping her eyes.

"What the hell is this?" I yelled. "John, what the hell is this? Where is my sister!"

"What do you mean?" He asked, wide eyes on me. "This is Rosa. She's right here."

They stared at me with those blank eyes. And when she was quiet, when she was calm, that teenager looked exactly like Rosa. Only it wasn't my Rosa, staring at me with those horrible vacant eyes. Then she smiled. Even her smile was exactly like her.

"No," I said.

"Yes," John said. "This is Rosa."

"Laura," the teenager with Rosa's face said. "Silly thing, you should have just knocked."

"No, no, no!" I stared down at my shaking hands. I could see where she'd scratched me, where she'd pulled at my clothes. That wasn't my sister. That woman wasn't my sister. "What have you done with Rosa?! You bastard!" I dove at him, hitting him with my fists.

The girl with my sister's face fell to her knees and started screaming, covering her ears. He stumbled backwards, trying to restrain me.

"What did you do to her?! What did you do?"

I felt something jab into the side of my neck. I could see my hands wavering in front of my face, clawing at his lab coat. I could see his expression, a smile that shifted like water. Then everything went dark.

*

My head stung. Then it felt numb. Then it was less than that, like being nothing at all.

"Rosa, it was always Rosa."

It was like I was deep within myself, too far from the surface to see through my own eyes.

"I mean, you know how it is. She's everything to you as well."

"John . . . John, I don't . . ."

That voice didn't sound like mine. It was faint and weak like all the air had been slowly pulled out of me. Like I was floating or not quite there.

"Rest now."

Something sharp.

Warm.

*

My face is in bandages. I hate the smell, like a chemical cleaner. My hands are bandaged as well. I can't move them. I'm strapped down to a dentist's chair.

The lights are dimmed, but it's too bright.

"Ah, your eyes are open."

The chair faces the wall, so I cannot see when he comes in. John switches on the light, and I clench my eyes shut as stinging pain wraps around the top of my head and squeezes like a vice. I want to scream. My face is numb, and the sound I produce is unintelligible.

"Sorry, too bright?"

The lights dim a little, and he settles down on a chair in front of me.

"Sorry, Laura, I imagine you must be very uncomfortable." He smiles. "The bandages need to stay on for a little longer. But don't worry, this won't be forever. Not at all." His hand touches my jaw, and I'm horrified that I can't squirm away, can't flinch. I can't do anything to show my discomfort.

He sees it in my eyes.

"You know, this might be the first time we've talked where you haven't said something rude." He holds up a little light and shines it in my eyes. My eyes water, and I'm unable to flinch. I lie there, dazed and upright. "Well, everything seems fine. I'm going to put you out again. Get some rest. You'll be recovered soon."

The sound I make is humiliating and inhuman.

"Didn't catch that," he says, and I want to scrape my nails across his eyes. "Here we go, little sting, then it's time to sleep."

*

My sister is playing with her toy ponies while I make us pasta. Our parents are at a party. Martiza is staying over at a friend's, and Beni is playing video games unhelpfully upstairs. I ask Rosa to pass me the cubes of cheese I prepared earlier. She balances the cubes on the back of her pink pony and carefully gallops them over to me.

My sister is crying. Her friends have fallen out with her over her scented jell pens. They wanted her to share, and she knew they wouldn't give them back. She curls up on my bed because it's tidier and cries for ten minutes until I bring her tissues and a glass of orange juice.

Rosa is watching some horrendous cartoon about a troll that likes gardening while I do my homework. She looks up at me and smirks as she says, "That's YOU in this," about the hideous troll queen whenever she comes on.

"Yeah?" I say, "Well, that's YOU in this." I point at the pig-nosed little boy on screen.

"No! No! It's not!" she shrieks.

*

"Where is my sister?"

He is trying to pour water down my throat.

"Have a drink first."

I let him give it to me and repeat myself.

"Where is my sister?"

"She is with us," he said.

"Show her to me."

"She isn't ready yet," he said. "Trust me. She will be with us soon."

"My secretary knows where I am."

"Which is why you emailed him to let him know that you're staying here to look after Rosa," he said.

"No."

"You're fine. It's fine. I'm a doctor."

"I want to see my sister. What have you done to me?"

"Stop now, don't upset yourself."

*

Rosa tells me that she is going to leave him. She's packed a bag. She's made up her mind. I have a room prepared and set up for her. I bought blue sheets, she has always liked blue. I tell her that I can come and pick her up. Rosa tells me no; she wants to talk it all out before she leaves him.

Days later, she'll tell me that she loves him, that if she was to leave, it would be like crushing her heart into pieces. She tells me that I've never wanted someone like that. She is right. She sounds mentally ill.

We argue.

Months later, we meet at a dinner for Martiza's birthday, and she tells me she's sorry. We hug. I ask if she's happy, and she says, "Like never before."

*

He unbandaged my legs first. From how I was strapped, I couldn't see them. But I could feel how he touched me, hands pressing, intimate, not like a doctor. I lie there and crave the ability to kick his face in, mash it into meat on the ground.

"There, good as new," he said, one hand running along my thigh.

"Where is my sister?"

There is something sad in his eyes, I realise when I ask.

"In a way," he said, "you only have yourself to blame for what happened." He met my eyes. "You were always trying to keep her away from me." He ran his palms along the skin of my thighs before standing up and taking hold of an arm. "It was a year after we got married. We were fighting, it was all normal stuff. But you told her that it wasn't."

I can see my arm as he is unravelling it. I had a scar on that arm from when I broke it as a child. I had a scar on that arm. . . .

"So, I come home one night after a long day, working hard to put food on the table for my beautiful wife. And I find . . . and I find my beautiful wife waiting for me with a packed suitcase. And she told me she was going. She said all this ugly stuff to me, horrible things. And I knew, I knew you'd put her up to it."

He went quiet, hands shaking as he unwrapped my fingers one by one.

"We had a fight. She called me crazy. I tried to snatch the suitcase from her hands. We struggled, and she fell. She tripped and fell down the stairs of our apartment building. I rushed to her, but it was too late. Her neck had snapped like a toothpick."

His eyes filled with tears. "What was worse, this woman saw. She was our neighbour from downstairs. She heard us and came out of her flat to see what we were doing. Stupid nosey woman."

Snapped like a toothpick . . .

The world plummeted. I fell from my body as the ground disappeared beneath me.

"You killed her . . ."

"No, no, no. Well, in a manner of speaking, yes, my Rosa was gone. I . . . well, you must know how you'd feel if you lost her? But then, as that nosey fucking bitch came over. She was yelling something. I couldn't hear her. But when I looked up, she stopped being the neighbour, and it was like my Rosa was in front of me again."

"You bastard—"

"No, no, no, no, no," he said, strapping my arm back down. "No. It was like Rosa had just moved from one body to another. The neighbour became my Rosa. She became your Rosa, really."

"I would have known. I would have known."

"Well, I know my own lovely wife's face well enough to recreate it. I knew every bit of her. We're soul mates. So that nosey woman became Rosa in body as well as spirit. I knocked her down and turned her into everything I knew she wanted to be. And it was hard. I mean, she kept crying, telling me I was crazy. I had to strap her hands down because she kept trying to destroy her lovely face."

"I would have known!"

My wrists sting from the bindings as I try and pull myself free.

"I would have known! You fucking pig!"

"Well, you didn't!" He snarled, gripping my bandaged face. "You're arrogant enough to think you're the only one who knew her—I knew her. She was my wife!" He squeezed, and my numb face began to ache. "I had to show her who she was. Made her learn about herself, learn about you, your family. I even showed her how to be with me. Just like we were."

"You're a liar!" My eyes stung as I cried. "You're lying!"

"Her name was Gloria McKenzie. She was twenty-seven, and she was my Rosa until she died about two years ago. We were pregnant; she was so excited." He began to unravel the bandages around my neck. "But then she lost the baby. It couldn't be helped. But it hurt her. Rosa was so sad, but then she started to change. She wanted to be Gloria again. She'd had enough."

"What have you done?"

"And she was going to tell you. I mean, you'd been a big sister to her for four years. Always nagging her about me. Looking after her. She wanted to tell you. She packed a bag. She hit me. She actually hit me. She went crazy. I hated stabbing her like that. It was self-defence. Who knows what she was capable of? She wasn't Rosa anymore."

I knew it. I knew it . . .

I could hear my heart pounding in my chest. I knew why I was at this angle, backed up, unable to see my body.

"After her, I panicked. You called and called. I told Martiza that Rosa was sick. She trusted me. Why did they all trust me except you? It terrified me, but I went to work, the same as ever. I found a model. A teenager. She came to me to get her breasts done. I took her for dinner instead. She was flattered. Stupid. Easier to control than Gloria had been. I drugged her, operated on her. Convinced her that she was my Rosa, the same as ever."

"I would have noticed . . ."

My heart was breaking. I hadn't noticed. She had seemed strange, but I hadn't . . . I hadn't even suspected.

"You didn't." He digs his fingers painfully against my throbbing temples. "You accepted her as Rosa the same way I did, the same way your parents did. But after a while, that vain little brat started to flag. She'd say I made her look old out of the blue—one time, she said it in front of your mother, and I froze. She was giving us away. Older than sixteen, sure, but I'd turned her into the most beautiful woman in the world!" His nails dug into my head, gripping my hair. "Can you imagine someone so ungrateful?"

He caught his breath.

"Then, I come home one day to find my Rosa, my beautiful wife, fucking some kid. Fucking some stupid teenage boy in my bed. In our bed! My Rosa wouldn't have done that. My Rosa wasn't some cheap woman. And so, I had to get rid of them. Both of them. After that, it was too hard to stay in the city. I found another girl, Carmen, you've met actually. She became Rosa. And she did the whole thing so well, you actually believed that we'd moved to the countryside."

Where was she?

"Carmen was the best so far. But country life didn't agree with her. I bought us here so she wouldn't have to focus on all that. I didn't want her to see pictures of that boy I killed. I wanted a fresh start. So, I started my clinic, my practice, a new life for us. She got to keep Rosa's little shop, and we were happy. Six months of marital bliss. But then you got involved again, always you, and suddenly my Rosa wanted to stay in the city." He rolled his eyes as he started unravelling my face. "I said no, of course. Of course, I said no. And then she began to fall to pieces. She found somewhere to take drugs. I know, in a small town like this, even here, you can find ways to hurt yourself like that. She became ... unstable, ugly, she'd get things wrong. My Rosa never would have polluted her body like that."

"She wasn't yours."

"She was. She is."

His fingertips run lovingly along my cheekbones as the bandages come off.

"You keep messing things up for me. But I found a solution. I mean, we won't even need the training materials, the family history, the quizzes on her favourite things or anything," he said brightly, stepping back. "You already know Rosa, like the back of your hand. You're perfect. Now the two of you get to be together forever."

The mirror is lifted, and I can see my sister's face staring back at me. I move my face, and hers matches my movements.

I see her face fill with horror and disgust as I feel bile rising in my throat, burning me up.

The tears fall down her face—my face—her face . . .

Hers . . . all hers . . .

He puts the mirror away.

He touches me, one hand on my cheek.

"There you are, Rosa."

A MUNDANE REBELLION

When did you become so stale? Maybe it's how you were born. Born stale and done. Sure, when you're a child, they tell you that the world is your oyster, you marvel at how special you are, and how you and everyone you know has something that makes them equally special and unique.

And you're a child, so you believe them, I mean, why wouldn't you? So you study hard, you work hard; you do what everyone else does and what everyone else tells you. You grow up, going through all the proper channels only to discover that no, sorry, the world is not your oyster. It never was.

Your studying leads you to break your back to get a job that bores the bones out of you. Your life follows a very dull pattern. Nobody cares who you are. You are not special or unique. You bring the cash in, just like everybody else. So you save and spend your hard-earned money on the things society expects of you: a roof over your head, bills, food, social expectations, etc. And it all adds up. You live paycheque to paycheque.

Sure, some people don't live like that. Some people go on to become successful actors, playwrights, writers, artists—but now, it's the 21st century; you only get that big by being squeezed out of the entry point of one of their own. You can kid yourself if you like, try and make it for a year or two, but it won't happen. You'll end up getting some crappy job to cover the cost of living, and boom, you're not a sales clerk/actor. You're just a sales clerk. Maybe a supervisor if you play your cards right. Nothing you do matters unless you *really* mess it up.

Unlike when you were a child, time starts speeding up. Years go by, and nothing changes. Your life is boring to live—imagine trying to describe it to someone else? You were never *special*. Look to your left, there are a hundred more of you, ready to take your place.

So you stay in your time loop of monotony, buying shit the media tells you that you need, to make that place you got a mortgage to pay for less of an empty soul-crushing hovel. And hey, let's say you meet someone who lessens the boredom. Someone who stays when the others didn't. And you might fool yourself into thinking that this makes you special as well.

Are you kidding me? The whole damn planet has always been full of people who thought they were important because someone else, who didn't matter, said they loved them.

Deep down, you know that two people can't understand each other completely—even as mundane as you are. And that could be enough for you, couldn't it? Just to find someone—who doesn't really understand you—to make your pointless life all better?

Oh wow.

And then, say you have kids. You might think that this gives your life some value. Or, fool you, you might think that this makes your kids special—all full of hope and promise like you used to be. But your kids aren't any different. Well done on breeding more worker bees for the mundane chain. Your kids will grow up and live the same boring life as you, if they're lucky.

You see other people laughing and talking, and it's like they don't even know how pointless they are. It pisses you off because now you have thought about this whole thing a lot. You stay up at night thinking about it. You close your eyes, and you even dream about it. So why do they get to be so damn happy just because they are too fucking stupid to see it?

I mean, look at you, you've got it all figured out, and you're miserable! Doesn't that seem a little unfair?

Eventually, you start thinking, 'How do I break this mundane cycle? How do I make this world a more interesting place for me?'

And honestly, it's very easy once you use your imagination.

So today, things are going to be a little different. Sure, you get up at the same time, brush your teeth, get dressed, have something for breakfast, etc. You're on your way to your tedious job. It might seem like any other morning. Or is it?

Spoiler alert, you packed a big screwdriver in your bag today. Let's see how this mixes stuff up.

You park your car and start walking to the office. At the corner by the big post office, you see this guy. He is just the worst. He's loud, garish, and walks with his hand down the front of his trousers. He's laughing down the phone to his friend about getting bladdered and fighting with some guy the night before.

Or, he is, before you wedge the screwdriver through his throat. It's a nice, smooth motion, like cutting through cheese. In and out. He gasps, and it comes out in a staggered wheeze.

You wipe the screwdriver on your coat and leave him on the ground.

See, even walking to work can be exciting!

You pop the screwdriver back into your coat pocket and decide to go get a coffee. The little place across the road from your office is always open at this time. You're stood waiting at the counter as the barista chats with this woman. This girl is literally talking over the top of you. It's not about much, some gossip about Jason and the lads. You stand waiting for her to come and take your order. She carries on chatting for five minutes before finally acknowledging you. You just stand there, smiling, though the excitement is killing you.

She takes your order; you're practically shaking with glee. She tells you to have a nice day as she hands you your coffee, and you jab the screwdriver through the soft part of her face.

Unable to see you (at least from one eye) through all the blood, she falls to the ground, howling in agony. You walk away with your coffee, humming cheerfully to yourself. Hell, she clearly didn't want to be at work today. Now she can take some time off.

You manage to edge the severed eyeball from the end of the screwdriver. It makes a small popping sound as it falls, root and all, to the floor. You put it by the napkins and sugars so nobody steps on it.

By the bus stop near your office, a gaggle of teenage boys are shoving each other, laughing at how loud and obnoxious they can be, while the small gaggle of commuters by them stand by awkwardly. The boys find it especially hysterical when one of them nearly falls into one of the tired, waiting adults.

A double-decker bus is coming by. It's the number 18. It doesn't stop here.

You step forward and shove one of the boys out in front of it. There is a scream, a screech of tyres, and a sound not entirely dissimilar to a cat going for a spin in the washing machine. The surviving boys stand in shocked silence as they know the game will no longer work with just two of them.

Ah, into the office you go! You say hi to Mike at reception. He is nice enough not to say anything about your attire. The elevator is broken again. How annoying. Looks like it's the stairs for you. Careful, they are a tad slippery this morning! It's because of all the blood on your shoes. Watch your step now. Woah there, champ.

Now you're ready for another dull day, punching numbers and getting emails from that witch upstairs who hates your guts. Now that lady is a piece of work! Whether it's imposing deadlines that touch on the impossible or having you stand there while she writes on a piece of paper what she had just told you a moment ago, or spelling your name wrong in every email she has ever sent you.

In fact, today you're expected to get her some data before ten o'clock that requires you to use four different programmes and cross-compare two spreadsheets. She gave you this deadline yesterday as you left the office.

But that was yesterday. Today you're not accepting the same old, same old. So, since you're on a roll, why not poke your head around her door this morning and give her what for? It's just one more floor, go on.

You leave a smudge on the door when you knock. She barks at you to come in. Same as usual. You stand in front of her desk while she finishes her phone call. It's a personal call. Then as she's finishing up her goodbyes, her eyes flicker over to you. First in irritation, then a different expression comes over her. She drops her mobile and just stares at you.

"Hi, Cameron," you say. "It's about that task you gave me yesterday as I was leaving. I just wanted to suggest shifting it back until tomorrow. I know you probably remember from your days downstairs, but gathering that kind of data really takes some time."

She doesn't speak. Her mouth falls open like a kind of mournful goldfish.

"Was that a nod? A nod? I think it was!" You clap your bloodied hands together and offer her a cheerful smile. "Excellent, well, I'll keep you updated, of course!"

As you sit down at your desk, sipping your morning coffee, you rejoice in your mundane free morning. Punching numbers isn't so bad, you guess. You check your emails; nothing special. You make a phone call to marketing. You fix up that spreadsheet that your colleague left in a mess. You print the documentation you need for that meeting this afternoon. Today is a great day.

You're debating making a cup of tea when you hear the sirens.

Best set your email to 'Out of office.'

SLEEPLESSLY SLEEPWALKING

My sister is sleeping. Our parents say she
might never wake up. She just lies in her
bed, attached to machines that beep in the
background.

Beep. Beep. Beep. Beep.

The machines and tubes look painful, but my
sister is perfectly serene while she sleeps.

She doesn't move. Her eyes are closed, and her
hands and feet are still. My mother goes and
sits by her bed in the evening. She brushes the
hair out of her eyes and reads her stories. The
doctor said that it is good to speak to her as she
may be able to hear us.

That was where the problems started. You see,
because we are twins, people have . . .

. . . Always assumed closeness.

You see two young sisters with the same face,
and you think, 'They must be best friends.'

Wrong.

If you paid the slightest bit of attention, which adults never do—you would see two identical girls, sure. One who's captured everyone's attention and hearts—all the while being completely rotten to the core.

And at her side, you would see her timid shadow. Someone lonely and awkward and utterly paralysed by childish threats like, 'I'll tell Mum and Dad.'

We did everything together.

That was how she liked it. Trips into town, to the beach, to the arcade. This town is small, and we stood out. Cute twin girls, presumably best friends, why not? We were always together. The one time I left her alone . . .

The only time I stood up to her . . .

A paperboy found her. She had tumbled from the cliff she wanted us to climb together and bashed herself to pieces on the sand below.

Not killed, fleeting brain activity, two broken legs, a shattered wrist, seven broken fingers, four broken ribs. While the doctor spoke to my parents, I sat at her bedside and stroked her hand.

"I hate you," I told her. "I hope you never ever get over this."

Then, a month later, she came home and now just lies there, still and peaceful, almost like she's dreaming. And yet, I am uneasy. There are times where I see a shadow moving out of the corner of my eye, or it feels like someone is stood behind me.

"I'll tell Mum and Dad what you did."

Beep. Beep. Beep. Beep.

I look up, spin around and see her asleep across the hall.

I keep my door closed at night. The beeping of the machines freaks me out. It doesn't help much, I mean, it's just a door, but it's something. Or it was. Just recently, the beeping has gotten louder and louder like the *Tell-Tale Heart*. I remember reading that story for the first time. I was so frightened. I think about it now whenever I close my eyes.

Beep. Beep. Beep. Beep.

But the beeping of machines are the least of my problems. You see, even though I know my sister is plugged in, rigged up, unconscious, unmoving. Even though logic tells me that it just isn't possible, I see her moving around at night. A giggle in the darkness, the scrambling of feet on the carpet.

Once I got up to pee, and I heard someone running around outside the bathroom door, dashing backwards and forwards across the landing like we used to when we were little and afraid of the dark.

Beep. Beep. Beep. Beep.

Something scratches my door at night. Nails running high along the wood, higher than

either of us could reach. They scrape along the
top of the frame. A voice calls my name.

"Let's go to the cliff," it crows. "I know the
perfect spot. Open the door, come on."

It's like her voice, but not. It's like a chill
ripping up inside me. It's the feeling that makes
the hair stand up on the back of your neck.

She is outside my door, scratching and
whispering. And I can't move. I can't open the
door. I don't want to see her on the other side,
staring at me and waiting.

Beep. Beep. Beep. Beep.

Always until the morning comes. It's the only
thing that makes her go away for sure.

He hasn't come to see her. The man she said
she loved. The man, because that's what he is.
It's disgusting. He hasn't given this a second
thought.

That man who smelled of cigarettes—who
she made us go and meet in the dark, dark
apartment on the outskirts of town.

I suppose if he did turn up . . .

It would just look suspicious. What would Mum
and Dad think? Their teenage daughter being
associated with a grown man?

She met him on one of those nights we told
Mum and Dad we were at a friend's house when
actually we donned makeup like war paint and
snuck into one of those down-town clubs that
don't ID properly.

Those places frighten me. They always have,
and I can't imagine a time when they won't.

Flashing lights, sticky floors, the stench of
booze and sweat. Hands grope, bodies grind
against you. And men stare; they stare like they
want to hunt you down and rip you to pieces.
My sister loved it there, and me and whichever
girl from our class she had roped into joining us
would hold back and try our best not to show
how scared we were.

She asked him for a cigarette outside, away
from the music.

It began there. Everything that happened and
everything happening now, it all started in that
instant.

Nails rake along the wood, and then, as
sunlight starts to flicker through the blinds,
she finally stops. The scratching stops, and I
just know she's gone. Until tonight.

I open the door, and she's back in her bed,
sleeping.

Beep. Beep. Beep. Beep.

My life is now a matter of getting through the
night. By day, I put myself through the motions,
try to catch some sleep where I can. I am
supposed to be enjoying my life without her.

People avoid me in school. I think they have
been told to give me some space. My parents
let me stay home if I want. The option is always
there, they say. I don't want my nightmares to
follow me into a public place.

Sometimes, I think about going down to that
dark, dark apartment on the outskirts of town.

I'd wear one of her dresses, knock on the door
and scare him shitless.

He made her worse, so much worse. He let her
loose on her sadistic side.

He made her needy, wild, and cruel.

Everything she always had the potential to be.

After school, we would go home, eat dinner,
and go to bed. Then we'd get dressed and sneak
out. We did it every night—to a club or end up
cramped in his car or back at his flat.

"Your sister doesn't know how to have fun," he
said to her. "You two look exactly the same, but
she just sits there with a face on." He kissed her
neck, looking over at me as he spoke.

"Oh, she hardly knows how to function unless I
tell her what to do," she said, prodding his head.
"Hey! We look *exactly* the same? You mean you
can't tell us apart?"

He laughed and scooped her onto his lap. "Well,
I bet you'd look different if you stripped."

The others laughed. They were all guys, all
older than us. When they laughed, you could
see all of their teeth, sharp, like predators
about to eat.

My sister wasn't scared. She just rolled her
eyes.

"Wow, wouldn't you like to know?"

He was whispering in her ear, laughing that
low laugh of his, one big hand on her thigh.
My sister chugged back her beer before
adding, "Well, Kimi does have this super cute
birthmark on her back. It's in the shape of a
heart. I'm so jealous."

"That's adorable," he said. "Hey, Kimi, give us a
peek."

There are times I see my face in the mirror, and
for a moment, I am so sure she is staring back
at me, looking at me through my eyes. I start to
go into a panic. It rises up inside me like bile.
My hands shake, and I have to look away.

It's like she follows me in the day but cannot
make a move until it gets dark.

Every night, I go to bed with a heavy heart. I
listen to my mother reading to her, talking to
her.

"We all miss you," she says.

I think about unplugging her machine once
our mother goes to bed. I could pretend it was
an accident. We could all pretend it was an
accident.

When you are somebody's slave, you start to
obey them even when you don't want to. That is
their power.

I refused that day to go climbing, but the
aftermath was Hell.

I had started walking back towards the cliff to
see if she was ok.

That was when I saw her fall.

That was when I went to hide in the bathroom. I said I felt sick and locked myself in. I listened to the music that made my head spin. I listened to the way they all laughed like a pack of hyenas.

I waited and waited for the music to go out, to hear people say their drunken goodbyes.

Her nails raked on the door frame. Only I let her in.

"What the fuck is wrong with you?" she asked.

Her eyes were out of focus, and she swayed as she sat down to use the toilet.

"Those guys freak me out. Sis, it's so late. I want to go home."

Her eyes focused on me and narrowed like I had said something disgusting.

"I'm having fun. Go home if you want, but if you leave me alone, I'll tell Mum and Dad that you snuck out tonight."

My fear of those predatory eyes toppled with my old fear of her exposing me.

"You came here too," I said. "If you tell on me, it'll expose both of us, and you'll never see that creep again."

"You're a pathetic little virgin. Who do you think Mum and Dad will believe? I can lie at the drop of a hat. You'll stammer your way through the truth. Imagine how that conversation will go."

She tugged up her underwear and smoothed
her dress down.

"Have fun hiding in the toilet like a baby."

She slammed the door behind her, and I jumped
up to lock it again.

"Are you feeling okay?" My mother put a hand
on my forehead. "You look feverish."

"I'm fine." I eye the storybook under her arm.
It's a book of fairy tales we used to read as kids.
"It was a long day at school."

Sleeping in the nurse's office for two hours,
mumbling something about Mimi made it
easier for me to get out of her calling my
parents.

When I dream, I dream about a single
door, alone in a field of corn that overlooks
a thousand stars. It always begins
peacefully, but soon I start to feel anxious
as I stare at that door. I want to open it
and see what lies on the other side. But
whenever I get close, all I feel is waves of
anxiety and—

She climbed the cliff to the ridge at the top
where you can see the ocean. It's beautiful up
there.

She climbed all the way by herself. So far and
high, and I started to climb up after her—

The tapping of nails on the door, waking me
from half-sleep. A hand on the doorknob,
twisting it, shaking it.

Those words.

"I hope you never wake up."

The door starts to open, so I climb out of the
window. Feel the cold glass of the conservatory
roof beneath my feet as I slide down. It comes
easily; we have been sneaking out for years now.

I look up as I land on the ground.

My sister is staring down at me from our
bedroom window.

So I run.

She is lying face down on the sand, broken
limbs around her. I watch from up above and
eventually begin climbing back down.

She was lying face down on that grimy bed. He
was laughing and smoking with another guy
who was doing up his trousers. The room smelt
of sweat and vomit.

"Are you still here?" he said, surprised.

His friend left, and I start trying to set my
sister up to dress her.

"We all thought you'd left."

I ignored him, struggling to put her underwear
back on. One leg and then the second.

He grabbed my arm and forced me away from
the bed.

"Hey, I'm talking to you. What do you think
you're too good to talk to me?"

His breath stank.

"Get off me."

"You're a frigid bitch. Thought you'd be fun like your sister, but I guess the similarities stop at your face."

I yanked my arm free. His hands left red marks on my skin.

"Was she conscious when you and your friend had a go?"

My tone made him fluster. Then he just sneered. "Why? You jealous?"

"You make me sick. We're leaving now."

When I turned my back, he grabbed me again. He slammed my face into the wall. As I struggled and started yelling, he ripped open my dress at the back.

"Calm down, princess," he said, still laughing, grinding my nose into the wall. "No need to get excited. I just want to see that little heart on your back."

I started screaming. I tried to kick him, but the dress came off anyway. He forced me onto the ground, tugged at my tights, still laughing, now at my childish underwear.

"Now, where's that birthmark?"

His breath reeks as he gets down on top of me. His fingers pinch like a vice on my legs and chest. He sinks his teeth into my shoulder. That's when I started crying. He turned me

around, and I start hitting his face, scratching
at his body. His hand reaches down and grabs
my hair, he lifts my head high and then *slams* it
back into the floor. I hear my own scream, and
then I *hit* the ground again. He lifts me up, and
he *puts me down.*

And then it's like my body is made of clouds and
I just . . .

Float—

Float away from it.

I know there's something wrong.

I know there's something wrong.

But right now, my head is filled with clouds.

And I don't care.

Because my head is filled with clouds and I . . .

I feel like none of this even matters.

Like it doesn't even . . .

I woke up sore to the sound of muffled crying.
My head stung, but I sat up, and I saw him.
Jack was on top of me. Only that wasn't me. He
got up, and he was fixing the front of his pants,
and she was on the floor so still and so quiet.
And I found myself wondering—

Is that how I look when we're like that?

So still and so quiet?

And then she looked up at me. And I realised
how powerless I am. I vomited into the bedside

bin.

He got up and walked to me, patting my back as I got it all out of my system. He kissed me on the forehead.

"You two really are identical," he said. Then he ruffled my hair and slumped off to the bathroom.

She twisted up in a ball. Then she started crying. Really loud, frightened crying. She sounded like a baby or a little kid, and I felt repulsion in my chest like my heart was filled with lead. I hated him. I hated me. I hated her. I hated the bruises on her skin and that awful fucking crying. God, why wouldn't she stop? Please stop! Please!

I picked up her underwear and started pulling it onto her legs. Her tights were torn, so I left them there. I tugged her clothes onto her trembling body. She slumped, unmoving. So I slapped her face until her tears stopped. I put my jacket around her; her ripped dress didn't cover her much anymore.

As we waited for the 5am bus, she thanked me for the jacket.

"We share everything," I said, "Clothes, makeup and now apparently my boyfriend."

He called her a few more times after that. A grown man like him grovelling to a teenage girl for the *proper* twin experience.

It revolted her.

She blamed me because it was easy.

I wanted it to be like before. I never wanted
any of this. It made me feel sick and guilty, and
I hated feeling like that. Every day after, she
was suffocating me, always leaning over my
shoulder, always following me, and I couldn't
breathe!

So I—

                                           So she—

I didn't mean it. Not really. I went there to be
alone, and she followed me again.

               I wanted to talk about what happened. I wanted
                                 to speak to her—

I didn't ever want to talk about what happened.

I never even wanted to think about it again.

               So I climbed that cliff after her. I wanted things
                                 to be right.

She wouldn't listen to me.

                           She wouldn't hear me out.

She wouldn't go away.

                        She wouldn't even look at me.

So I pushed her.

I pushed her, and she tripped and she—

                                 And I—

Fell so hard and so fast.

               I knew I'd hit the ground. I saw her staring
                    down at me, shocked, scared.

And then she smiled.

And I kept falling.

It was like a door opened on the ground, and I
fell through the sky and into the stars.

She lay there, crumpled and crushed and small
like a puppet cut from its strings.

I swapped our bracelets. I told them it was
Mimi who fell.

She stole my name. I couldn't go back. She took
it all from me.

I have nothing left.

She is coming.

She is coming.

And I won't ever stop.

I know it's her crawling around in the corridors,
hiding in the mirror to scare me.

So I have to run.

I'll find her no matter where she runs.

My feet pounding on the pavement. I hear her
voice on the wind, carrying on the wind.

I hear her bare hands and feet tap-tap-tapping
on the ground.

Come here, Mimi. Don't you want to stay out
late?

Don't you want to stay out?

Leave me alone! Leave me alone! You're
suffocating me!

You ruined me.

It was meant to be better without you.

I am watching her climb the rocks, just like
that day. Watching her climb higher and higher
and higher.

She was never afraid of heights.

Now, neither am I.

Just like that day. I watch her staring up at me
from down there. She is stood on the exact spot
she fell to.

Her broken legs clicking and clacking back
together. Her face, just like mine, gazing up at
me.

She holds out her arms.

You see, just because we are twins, people
naturally assume closeness. You see two young
girls with the same face and think, 'I bet they'll
always be together.'

And you'd be right.

And you'd be right.

I'm coming.

But the Mouth Kept Screaming

On December 31st, Jonathon Lancaster had dismissed his three clerks at four. A treat for his hard-working team, as Mr Lancaster was not the type of employer to allow a second to be cut from the average work day. But as stern as ever, Jonathon ignored their rushed thanks, their bright smiles, their friendly chatter amongst themselves as they finished their work and put away their quills and ink for the day. He grunted in irritation as Nicole, the serving girl, called to him from the door to wish him a good evening.

A good evening indeed.

The clerks and Nicole would return home to their families, no doubt. He had heard them talking about plans to go to the tavern, cook dinners with their wives and husbands, or trips out of the city to their parents on the late evening train. Everybody had someone to return to tonight, except him.

Jonathon was sitting behind his desk, finishing off the last of his correspondences. His eyes were strained, exhausted from the long day. A shiver ran through him as the last of the embers in the grate started to grow dim.

That is quite enough for today, he decided.

He rose from his chair and put on his coat from the hook. With his letters in hand and his offices locked up for the night,

Jonathon stepped out into the brisk evening air. The streets were crowded and lively with late night revellers. He tucked his scarf into his coat as he broke in through the crowd. On occasion, it relaxed him to leave the office and settle in amongst the hustle and bustle of the busy Camden streets. However, tonight was not one of those times. It was a merry evening, too merry for him.

He sighed, rubbing his sore eyes again. There had been a time when all of these cheerful people wouldn't have phased him. Once, he would have left the office on New Year's Eve and had a carriage collect him from the door in his haste to return to his family. Yes, not all that long ago, when he would have returned to his wife and four children. Alas, no more. And his house seemed bare and cold without them, particularly around the holidays.

His daughter Margaret had married six months ago, to a husband who had taken her north to Manchester of all places. She was in a delicate condition already and had been unable to make the journey down to be with him for the annual celebration at their family's estate. Her apology had been too detailed to ring true for him, but Jonathon put those feelings aside.

His second son, James, had perished in a war abroad two years ago. His medal was all he had left of him. When he returned home, Jonathon would light a candle for him and watch the year 1890 arrive without his son.

His youngest child, Charles, was likely buried in some indecent establishment. The last time Jonathon had gone out of his way to find Charles, he had collected him from a derelict opium den and paid a handsome price for it as well. There had been promises then, tears that it would never happen again, but of course that was until the next time and the time after that. No, Jonathon was not willing to spend another New Year's Eve scouring the taverns and coffeehouses where his son went to dance with other men. He had given up on the notion of re-establishing his youngest into society.

He rubbed his gloved hands together to keep warm as the wind rushed through the air, knocking off the top hat of a man beside him. The young man cried out in alarm, hand outstretched, missing the brim of his hat by an inch, and in that second, he looked so much like . . .

No. Jonathon sighed. His eyes were playing tricks on him again.

For his eldest son, his Alexander, often haunted his thoughts. In the ten years since he had last seen him, Jonathon thought he'd spotted him a hundred or so times. He'd seen his son's cold green eyes in young men in the gutter, in the work-house, or dusted with soot in his factory. He always thought, or perhaps, he hoped. But it was never Alexander in the end. No doubt he would enter the new year without ever knowing what became of his Alexander.

The crowd around him began to slow. Jonathon grunted in irritation. Up ahead, he could hear the tinkering of bells, and someone singing—begging for coins no doubt. A spectacle that would distract every brainless soul from going about their business. He pushed his way past a large woman with a feathered bonnet and stepped into an alleyway to try and cut past the street performers. He was in no mood to part with his wallet by passing some gipsy child or musical bloody vagrant.

Smoothing his jacket, Jonathon stalked through the back streets, muttering in irritation.

At least, he would soon be home. There was a bottle of brandy he had been saving. The perfect companion to see in the new year, now that his ungrateful children had all grown away from him. He turned a corner and passed a beggar with a tattered coat and a small, dirty brown hat left out in front of him. Jonathon winced, covering his mouth with his hand as he passed, the smell of urine drifting unpleasantly from the unfortunate creature.

"Spare any change, sir," it croaked.

He cast his gaze down. The man before him looked about his age with skin so filthy, he could scarcely work out his features.

A beard matted and likely riddled with lice, and blackened hands and feet.

"Do you have no gimmick?" Jonathon asked curtly. "No song or dance to exchange for my copper piece?"

"I would, sir," he said, "but I'm afraid I don't quite have the strength."

"Ah, a sad tale for my trouble," he said coldly. "I'd work on something more convincing. Good day." He strode past him and back out onto the main street. The crowd seemed to have slowed down now, and Jonathon dusted himself off as he continued down the high street towards the carriages.

He was ready to go home. 1889 had been long enough for him.

*

The carriage driver was quiet and efficient, a little blessing at the end of his day. Jonathon had taken the journey to rest his eyes and try to leave some of his city stress back in Camden where it belonged. He had little to no opportunities to relax and unwind, so his travel in and out of the city was precious to him. Peace and quiet were, so often, just out of his reach. Though, he reasoned, there would be plenty of that tonight. He wouldn't begrudge the staff holding their little celebrations in their quarters, but he would see in the new year alone in his chambers. Unless, for whatever reason, Charles had managed to dig himself into such trouble in the city that he had to venture home.

Jonathon rubbed his cold face irritably at the thought.

Of course, his sister Penny had invited him out to her own celebrations in Surrey. Although he could scarcely stand the thought of spending the night with Penny's banker husband, Percival, who had a penchant for falling asleep mid-sentence. Additionally, Penny and Percival's collection of friends all fell into the type who found the weather to be a thoroughly engaging topic of conversation and would, no doubt, whittle away his sanity with their dry talk.

"It's like they passed away several years ago but were too dull to realise this was the case," Melody had said to him once.

He chuckled aloud at the memory, causing the carriage driver to startle and glance over his shoulder at him. Jonathon coughed and gestured with his hand for the man to continue. Inwardly, he cursed himself. It would do him no good to think of *that woman* tonight. She needed to remain under lock and key in his brain as she was in life.

Wincing to himself, Jonathon wondered if he had been as obvious to Penny about his excuse for not coming along to her festivities tonight as his own daughter had been in hers to him. He liked to think he was a better liar than Margaret, who even as a girl, would go white as a sheet when she wavered with the truth. It was a skill he had perfected as a school boy, improved as a lawyer, and one he had been sure to never pass on to his children.

"Here we are, sir," the driver called to him as they reached the front gates.

"To the door, please."

As the collection of glass and bricks came up to meet him through the carriage window, Jonathon felt that familiar pang of unease in his belly. His stomach twisted uncomfortably, and he took a long, heavy breath to recover himself.

When did I start to dread this place? Jonathon thought. *When did that happen?*

As a boy, it had always been his favourite place in the world. He had learned to read in this house. He had learned to ride and shoot on these very grounds. And when he was sent away to school, the Lancaster Manor was the happy nest he always returned to during the holidays. When he married, he'd been excited to share this home with his wife, with his children. For the longest time, this was a place of great comfort to him.

Of course, it had changed since then. Try as he might to have repaired the damage, the west wing of the house still bore a scar from the fire. He could see it from here as he approached from the gates. Was it then that he began to hate returning home? Was it this scar on the face of the house that filled his guts with ice?

No. He could recall this feeling manifesting long before the fire.

Frowning, he reasoned that if he had to put an exact timeline on when this feeling began, it would have been just after James was born. Things had been demanding at the firm; he had been made partner, and his workload expanded to an unreasonable amount. He would return home exhausted after a long day. He had only wanted to come home to a bit of comfort. He expected a meal on the table, a smiling wife, quiet, well-behaved children. And yet more often than not, he came back to discover his family playing some make-believe game. His family home, the house he'd grown up in, ransacked. Toys and clothes strewn about the landing. Their children running around like a gaggle of stray dogs. And his *wife*, she was too wild, too silly to be a mother.

No matter how many times he'd tell her he didn't approve, how many conversations where he explained how badly it made their family look, *that woman* was incapable of understanding his point of view.

"Thank you," he said curtly to the driver as he stepped from the carriage.

"And a Happy New Year to you, sir," the man responded.

Ridiculous, he thought to himself as the carriage and horses worked around the gardens and back towards the front gates. Jonathon tucked his scarf tighter around him and he strode towards the front door. As he did so, he couldn't help but notice that the evening had grown colder. The wind had picked up, sending his overcoat spiralling around him and his scarf struggling to break free from the confines of his collar.

The old elm tree that had stood to the left of the house since Jonathon was a boy, creaked uncertainly. He looked up hesitantly at its bare branches as they etched and scratched against the blackened scar on the bricks. Then, out of the corner of his eye, Jonathon saw a trail of long silvery hair amongst the branches. He bolted backwards, staring up into the tree in the dim lamp light. There couldn't be someone up there . . . ?

The wind rushed down to meet him, and he was so sure, so foolishly sure, in that moment, that he heard the tinkling of laughter. A hand to his mouth, Jonathon blinked, trying to see better. The wisps of silver blonde trailed in the wind to be revealed only as a piece of string drifting down to land at his feet. Squinting now, he could see the thing in the tree better.

A deflated paper lantern, he realised on closer inspection. From the servants' silly celebrations and nothing more.

Jonathon cursed himself for being stupid and climbed the steps to his door, letting himself inside. He really needed that drink to put such dimwitted thoughts behind him for good.

Over the years, he had always kept a small staff at Lancaster Manor. His own father did not believe in wastefulness when it came to maintaining a household. Mrs Mills, the housekeeper, had been at her post for some twenty years and she understood well how to manage things here. McClish, the gardener, who was so old, he had been with the Lancaster family since before Jonathon himself was born, and his son, Mathias, who managed the dogs. The butler, Henry, had been taken on to replace that dreadful creature Melody had brought with her from her girlhood home. Henry was quiet, efficient and there was little more Jonathon required for such a position. The cook, his valet Robert, and the balding footman had all been here since the fire. Then there were three silent maids whom he suspected Mrs Mills rotated on a fairly frequent basis as he was never certain as to their appearance.

He informed Robert that he would take his dinner alone, with a brandy, in his study and was not to be disturbed. He dumped his coat and scarf with one of the maids and traipsed up the stairs to lock himself away.

*

His mother had been an admirer of French art. When he was a boy, their home had been decorated with landscapes and

portraits from these foreign painters. She'd owned several
Gilles Allou pieces, an a Boucher she had particularly loved. It
was her passion, and his father had tolerated it in abundance.
Jonathon hadn't much cared for it. Even as a boy, he had been
incredibly serious. His world revolved around his lessons and
riding. So, when the manor became his own, the portraits and
artistic pieces were taken to the attic and shut away.

However, in his study, Jonathon kept a portrait of his family
that was painted when his children were still young. As he
could recall, it had been a nightmare to make them sit still for
it, particularly James, who'd been a rambunctious boy, always
fiddling with something and speaking out of turn. The family
portrait once hung in the dining room. It cost a pretty penny,
and he had been proud of it. However, after the fire, it turned
his stomach to look at it. So, it was taken and placed above the
grate in his study.

He kept a small photograph of James in his uniform on his
desk, taken before he left for Burma. His son had only been
eighteen. He looked younger. Had his mother been around, she
no doubt would have made a fuss. He cursed.

Why is it that I can't stop thinking about her tonight?

Jonathon took a sip of his drink, setting the photograph
back down. The brandy was cold and crisp on his lips. He
sighed, rubbing his forehead. Jonathon turned the photograph
onto its front and moved over to select one of his books from
the shelf on his right.

As he did, Jonathon tweaked the curtain to one side so he
could peer out of the window. It was pitch black outside now,
with only the lamps to illuminate the grounds. Squinting,
he could see a candle burning in the gardener's cottage. He
supposed Mathison or old McClish may still be up, waiting for
the new year perhaps.

The grandfather clock chimed in the hallway outside, calling
out for ten o'clock.

Just two hours to go, he thought.

Jonathon leant against the wall, taking another sip of his

drink. It settled warm in his stomach. He rested his head against the wall and took in the quiet house around him. Perhaps it was better like this. This quiet. This stillness. Just him and his family portrait to see in the new year, sans actual family, who would only disappoint him in one way or another.

He polished off his glass and walked back over to his desk and cabinet to top himself up.

It didn't matter how much he drank tonight.

Jonathon was about to resume his seat behind his desk and pick up a good book, when he heard something clatter outside. He got to his feet and strolled over to the window.

A branch, he reasoned. *Surely, just a branch.*

But as he listened out, he could hear no wind. It had died down. He scowled, pulling back the curtain to peer outside into the darkness. He noticed that the lamps outside the house had gone out.

Was that the usual practice?

Upon occasion, he did prefer to stay at his rooms in Chelsea during busy times of the year, so he couldn't be sure. But it didn't seem right for the servants to take out the lights. Particularly on New Year's Eve, when surely they would use them to stay awake? He squinted a little, peering out across the way to see that the candle light was still coming from the gardener's cottage.

It must have been a branch, perhaps dislodged from the roof having blown there earlier this evening. He was being foolish again. It was all those silly thoughts of string or hair when he came home. What utter rubbish. Jonathon went to close the curtain when he heard a bang from the fireplace.

Flinching, he turned his head to see the fire in the grate crackle to life, sending a small cinder onto the rug.

He shook his head, letting out the breath he had been holding. How easily rattled he was tonight. It must be the stress from this long year catching up with him, nothing more. Perhaps if Charles had been less irresponsible or Margaret less selfish or Alexander less evasive, then he might be able to get through tonight without any schoolboy stupidity.

Jonathon shook his head and turned to close the curtains.

Only, as he looked back out, he noticed that the lanterns below were lit, illuminating the grounds before him again. His brow furrowed. Now, that was odd. Those lights had been extinguished just moments ago. He had seen them. Surely, they couldn't have been lit again so quickly. The footman, a veteran just as his son would have been, walked with a limp from an old war injury. He could never, not on his best day, have brightened those lamps in less than a moment. There was no way.

How very unusual. Maybe, it had been a trick of the light? He must be tired, that had to be it.

Jonathon rubbed his eyes, trying to peer down the gap to see if anyone was wandering around down there. There was a figure out on the grounds. Jonathon looked up and spotted them, illuminated now by the lamps. A tall, slim figure all in white, almost like a bride. Only the veil was wrapped around their head, around and around, obscuring their face.

His stomach lurched.

Could it be one of the servants playing some sort of joke? A kind of inane costume?

No. He couldn't picture any of his staff behaving so thoughtlessly. It was beyond belief. It didn't happen here. He pulled back the curtain properly, staring out of the window. This was no trick of the light. There was somebody out there, all in white, walking slowly towards the house.

Jonathon stepped back and reached for the bell on the side of his desk to call Robert up to him but thought better of it.

He returned to the window, cursing. The lights had gone out again, the grounds dark. He rushed to the desk again and rang the bell frantically. He bent down and pulled opened the bottom drawer, taking out his pistol. Hands trembling ever so slightly, he loaded the bullets and held it tight to his side as he returned to the window.

The lights were back on and the figure in white was gone.

There was a knock at the door, and Jonathon felt his arm

jerk upright, pistol in hand, aimed at Robert, who stepped back.

"Is everything alright, sir?" he asked, startled.

Jonathon retreated, hands trembling as he set the gun back down. "Robert, there is somebody out on the grounds. And would you mind telling me what the problem is with the lamps?"

"The lamps, sir?"

"Yes, man! The lamps, the blasted lamps." He gestured to the window. "Somebody keeps turning the lamps off and on."

"Sir, I don't see how that could be the case." Robert walked over to the window, frowning as he peered through. "Sir, the lamps are lit. I can guarantee nobody has extinguished them. I know for a fact that William has been having trouble with his leg today. I will speak with him, but . . ."

"Speak with him," Jonathon snapped. "Do what you like. But I saw a figure out there, some fool dressed in white sheets. Which of the staff is likely to do that? Because I thought I had a staff of professionals, rather than a gaggle of jesters and players."

Robert's brow furrowed slightly. "Dressed up? No, sir, I was just in the kitchens and everyone was quite accounted for and dressed as they should be."

Jonathon walked to him, peering out of the window. It was true, the lamps were lit and the grounds clear, just dusted white with frost. Squinting, Jonathon couldn't see any footprints from where that thing had been stood. He rubbed his eyes, face near pressed against the glass to try and see. "But . . ." he said. "I was so sure."

"Sir," Robert said, "I will speak to William about the lamps. Would you like me and Henry to go out and see if there is anyone wandering the grounds? It would be no bother."

He frowned, not taking his eyes from the spot in which he'd seen the thing in white.

"No," he said, his voice small. "No. It's . . . it's quite alright. I'm sure it was a trick of the light. Perhaps my mind is . . . playing tricks on me." He dropped his pistol back down on his desk, brushing back his hair. "I'm sorry. I'm just tired."

"Did you want me to sort out your bed chamber for you, sir?"

"No," he said. "I can manage myself. No, I'm going to stay in here a while. Goodnight, Robert."

"Goodnight, sir. Please, do let me know if you need anything."

"Yes, yes, good night."

He fell into his chair with a thud, drawing his hands over his head. He let his breath come in and out, in and out, as he heard the door click shut. In his mind's eye, he could see the figure in white, veil like sheets wrapped around its head. It had to be a trick of the light, like the paper lantern in the tree. Just his mind playing him for a fool.

Seeing it filled his stomach with dread. Just like . . . just like . . . that night, so long ago. Before Charles was born. The very first time he felt real agony and fear at the thought of coming home to this place. He had waited outside, watching his wife and children. He had watched them for a little while, and for the first time in their life together, Melody hadn't seen him. She had carried on playing. She had a silk scarf he'd bought for her wrapped around her head like a bandana, paint strewn across her pale, pointed features. She carried a wooden sword and clashed blades with Alexander, who was wearing one of Melody's old velvet jackets. They were all laughing like the deranged—Margaret and James chasing each other in circles, filthy and savage like a pair of dogs.

It was a world where his family existed without him.

He had watched them and waited to be seen for so long, until Melody, panting and exhausted from her efforts, had raised her pretty head and spotted him.

"Oh! Children, look, it's Daddy! Daddy's home!" she had said, waving cheerfully.

And their children—his children had waved with her, without knowing why.

It unsettled him still.

Jonathon rubbed his eyes and stood up. He finished his glass in one and poured himself another. Hands still trembling, he walked over to the window. The lamps were lit and there was nobody there, just the grounds and the gates in the distance. He took a deep breath and closed the curtains.

It was all in his head. It was nothing at all.

*

Jonathon closed his eyes and opened them again, letting out a deep breath. An hour had passed, and the lamps outside had remained lit. Jonathon had pulled his armchair from its place at the fireside to perch by the window. He frowned, peering out through the curtains to check once more.

The clock had chimed for eleven, and there had been no sign of any visitor in white.

Perhaps it had been that footman after all? Messing around with the lamps, perhaps Robert had spared their master the details of his drunken antics. Perhaps what he'd thought he'd seen had been merely one of the maids in a clumsy attempt at a costume—and his reaction merely a result of his own paranoid mind. But there had been no footprints in the frosted ground. There was no sign that anyone had been there.

Jonathon poured himself another brandy and settled back into his chair. He scowled up at the portrait above the grate. His younger, painted-self glared back at him. Now, *that* young man would not have been impressed with any of this carry-on. No, he certainly would have considered him a silly old clod. His lip curled. Perhaps, he should have burned that painting to ash long ago.

He got to his feet and walked over to the fireplace. Setting his glass down on the mantel, Jonathon reached up and took hold of the golden frame at the sides and lifted it awkwardly from the hanging. He glanced up and flinched as he locked eyes with the painted ones of his long absent wife.

Bright brown and wild. The painter, Richardson, Richmond... Richet, some name like that, had captured those eyes very well. It was quite uncanny.

Jonathon's insides curdled, and he tucked the piece in

beside his desk, amongst his paperwork. He let out a sigh of relief, wiping his brow with his hand before straightening up. He would ask for Henry to take the thing to be burned tomorrow. That would start the new year properly. It was futile sentimentality that had him keep it in the first place. Why honour a space in his sanctum at home to ungrateful children who ran and hid from him?

Why indeed?

The wall space above the grate looked bare without it, but for the rest of the night, he couldn't stand those wild brown eyes following him around the room. He cast a contemptuous look at it, half concealed by a box of paperwork now. His family, as they had been long ago. Himself at the centre, Melody sat beside him, a baby Charles in her arms. Alexander stood to attention at his side, with Jonathon's own flat green-eyed stare. Margaret and James sat beside their mother, so young, so different then. The two of them looked well-behaved and sweet, but they had been the furthest thing from it. Back then, Jonathon could barely stand to work from home, their noise seemed to swirl around the house, around and around and around until he felt as though he were going mad.

"Maggie, Maggie, follow me!"

Jonathon froze. His heart started to beat louder than before, thundering against his ribs. He swallowed hard. This had to be another queer result of exhaustion. This *could not* be his children running up and down the stairs outside his study.

"James! James, wait!"

A shriek and a crash and something, somewhere, was broken. That was how it had been then. Always, always, just when he was in the middle of concentrating on something difficult. It was as if they knew, as if they were sabotaging him on purpose. He clenched his eyes shut and took a step towards the door.

"James!" A burst of laughter, a shout, and footsteps tapping along the stairs and then the hallway outside, back and forth. He could hear it so clearly now. Jonathon took another deep breath.

I'm going to walk over to the door, he thought. *I'm going to walk right there and open it. Nobody will be there on the other side. Certainly not my children. My daughter is in Manchester, my son is long dead in his grave. My son is long dead.*

He reached out and quickly forced the door open. Jonathon stared out into the empty corridor in front of him. The lights were out, and his shadow stretched long in front of him, illuminated by the lamps and the fire in his study. It was quiet and still and empty. He smirked to himself, shaking his head.

What was he doing? Jonathon glanced over his shoulder to look at his own disapproving younger face from the portrait. But his heart flew into his mouth when he saw the blasted thing was gone. Jonathon swerved around to face it. He rushed back to his desk to try and find it when he felt a pair of wild brown eyes watching him.

Jonathon fell to his knees in shock, a moan of horror escaping from his lips.

The painting he had so carefully tucked away to one side was back above the grate. His own flat green-eyed stare glaring. His children, missing, away, or dead, looking out. And her, *that woman*, all wild and bright, smiling down on him like some unholy thing.

"What the devil is this?" he cried. "Who's there?" He got to his feet, heart racing. "Answer me! Answer me, now!"

He took an angry step towards the painting, tensing as he reached out to take it down again. He met her eyes. Something about her made him want to stop. Jonathon lowered his arms and picked up his bottle of brandy.

"I'm going to burn you in the morning," he said coldly. "Enjoy your last night of tenancy." He picked up his oil lamp from the cabinet on his right. So much for spending the new year in his study. Clearly, that room was going to play all sorts of tricks on him before the night was through. Jonathon slammed the door behind him, drawing his dressing gown around him as he stepped out into the cold corridor. He closed his eyes, taking in a breath. The house was quiet. No doubt his servants were having their own celebrations down in the kitchens. He would leave them to it and take to his bed early.

At his age, another year meant nothing. It would, no doubt, be another year of Charles accumulating debts, another year of Margaret's terrible lies, of putting flowers on James's graveside, and seeing Alexander in the face of every street beggar he passed. And another year for *that woman* to rot in Willow's Asylum.

He climbed the stairs to his bed, swigging his brandy from the bottle and feeling the warm liquid settle his stomach. Jonathon pushed open his bedroom chamber door with his foot and stepped inside. Robert had set the fire already, ever the efficient man. He yawned, closing the door behind him, and dropped the bottle down at his bedside. Adjusting the lamp with one hand, the room grew brighter.

Unlike his study, he kept no part of his family in his own quarters. It had been reorganised for his comforts alone, no silly trinkets or pictures to occupy space wastefully. Once, when he shared it with *her*, she had kept such things, bottles of perfume and rouges out on the dressing table. It looked cluttered and had always irritated him, but as usual, Melody had an excuse. Jonathon dressed in his night shirt and settled down on the bed, taking another sip of brandy to try and calm his nerves.

He took a deep breath. It would be midnight soon. The beginning of a new year. He should at least try to relax before it began. He closed his eyes and winced as he saw her wild brown ones appear before him, a flash of light and there she was.

Leave me be, he thought. *Will you just leave me be?*

The problems with his marriage, he reasoned, had existed when he had that damned painting commissioned, though you couldn't tell so much in smears of paint and oil. No, in the portrait, they made quite the picture-perfect creatures.

Jonathon's own parents had married for advantage. The match had suited both of their families financially, and so it was made. Fortunately, they had gotten along well and had been perfect companions to each other right up until their deaths fifteen years ago. Similarly, his sister Penny had married for status, with her dry, dull husband offering her security and wealth that, as a second child and a woman, would have been difficult to otherwise obtain. But, he mused, he himself had both wealth and a career that allowed him to double it and double it again. What he had wanted in a wife was neither advantage or status. Penny had often taunted him for his fixation on pretty women when he was younger. She said all it took was good symmetry to turn his head.

That had been the case with Melody.

His head had been turned a number of times, but never like that. He'd seen her at a charity ball at Cavindash Place when he was a young man. She was from a good family, the sister of one of his friends from university. Though, had they met in different circumstances, he would likely have been interested in her anyway.

But it had been that night.

He had gone without his parents, without his sister. Archibald had introduced the two of them, and he'd been instantly smitten. He asked her to dance, and she teased him about his clumsy feet, his sweaty hands. But then, after, Melody had wandered away, without her chaperone, without those silly girls she used to surround herself with, without her devoted brother. No, she had strolled off into the gardens, all alone, and he had followed.

Jonathon coughed uncomfortably. Yes, perhaps he had been too rough with her, too demanding. But she knew well what she was doing. She wasn't as naïve as she'd acted at the time. Based on how flighty and wild she could be after they were wed, he suspected that her little play at seeming so innocent had been just that. A *play*. He also suspected that she had tried such an act on many a young man before, whose head she had turned.

But he could admit, even to himself, that it had been wrong of him to rip her dress the way he did. But she'd opened her mouth and screamed. She'd just kept screaming and screaming. He had to use something to silence that awful, damning sound.

He regretted it, how could he not? If he thought about it, the noise began again, piercing his skull. He regretted that. It had been shameful. He would not have wanted any of his own sons to behave like that—for his daughter to have suffered as he made her mother suffer. But it was in the past. What followed between him and his wife did not begin there! He would very likely have approached her father to ask for her hand based on how she'd turned his head alone, not just because of what he did to her on the grounds at Cavindash Place.

Besides, the two of them married before she began to show.

Penny said he should have known that she was the wrong sort then. Too wild and silly to be a wife. Too wild and silly to be a mother. When she turned their home into a blasted fairy kingdom, he should have known. When she snuck away from his colleagues at parties to whisper away with that wretched former butler, he should have known. He should have removed their children from her sooner.

After the fire she lit in the west wing, there was so little he could do for them. Melody had to be sent away, she had to be locked up, where she could no longer hurt him or his children again. His father had shut his own sister away at Willow's before, long ago, due to some funny business with his inheritance. It was a trusted establishment. Secure. No matter how he feared, how his mind could play tricks on him, like tonight, there was no way his wife would ever leave that place. There would be no way she could come here to this house again.

If the children didn't understand, well, there was so little he could have done about that. They had all been so young. Charles was scarcely more than four years old. How could they understand something so awful as their mother starting a fire in the library and then boarding herself in the nursery with them? She had wanted to kill them all. How was he, or anyone else, supposed to have that conversation with little children who missed their mother?

What else could I have done? He thought, scratching his brow and leaning back in his bed.

The clock chimed downstairs. *I've made it*, he thought. *I've made it through this long, long night.* Jonathon let out a sigh of relief as he got to his feet. He strolled over to the window to look outside. The moon was bright; he could see it now, out from behind the overcast clouds. The gardens now dazzled with frost completely. The world was still and white. A perfect new beginning for a new year.

Something flickered out of the corner of his eye. Jonathon tensed, watching his own reflection in the glass. It had been the slightest movement. He feared he'd miss it if he blinked again. Trying to keep his eyes focused, Jonathon watched as a trail of silvery blonde hair stuck out from beneath his bed.

When I turn around, he thought to himself, closing his eyes tightly. *There will be nothing there. There's nothing under the bed. This is a trick of the light. This is nothing. Count it down. 3-2-1-Open!*

And yet, when he went to open his eyes, he found he could not. Jonathon's hands started to sweat. His grip nearly slipping on the bottle. He let out a deep breath, trying to calm himself down. *3-2-1*, he repeated in his mind. *3-2-1-Open!* He opened his eyes and there was a hand, small and white and reaching out from under the bed, a trail of silvery hair in front, a head? Like someone was crawling out from underneath.

When I turn around, he thought to himself, *When I turn around, there will be nothing.*

He opened his eyes and the hand and the head trailing long, blonde hair was gone. He let out a gasp of relief, then the knocking started. Pounding on the door, frantic, hammering. He leapt back in alarm.

"Whose there?" he called. "Who the hell is there?"

The knocking persisted. Louder and louder, slamming on his door so hard that he feared the lock would break. Then it started above him. BANG-BANG-BANG! It was like someone was on the level above, pounding their fists against the floor. He cried out, heading towards the door.

"WHO THE DEVIL DO YOU THINK YOU ARE?" he called,

striding past the bed and reaching for the handle.

The knocking grew quiet. Hand trembling, he grasped the handle and went to twist it open, when the banging began again, rattling the door in its frame. Jonathon recoiled in shock, stepping back, drawing his hands over his mouth. He started to speak, so sure he had called Robert's name amongst curses and prayers. He stumbled and fell onto the bed with a thud. Heart now slamming against his ribs with such violence, he felt as though his blood was burning. He could hear running up the stairs. His children, Margaret and James, when they were young, shrieking with laughter as they ran. He covered his ears and drew the blankets over his head, willing the noise to stop.

"Melody," he groaned, "Melody, darling, is that you?"

He flinched as he felt hands on his shoulders, gentle hands, easing the blankets away from him, drawing him out. A chill ran up his body as he was exposed, and Jonathon realised to his horror, that the fire in the grate had gone out, that the lamp had been turned down completely. The room was bathed in moonlight.

But there it was. Stood just in front of the bed. The figure from the grounds. All in white, a sheet-like veil twisted around and around the head, covering the nose and the eyes, obscuring the face. Jonathon couldn't move. He stayed still, trying desperately to find the will to make a sound.

"Melody, is that you?" he whispered in a childish voice that seemed to have been lost to him for so very long.

The creature's mouth was exposed, just underneath where veil met sheet, leaving a horrible wide gash of a mouth. It was smiling at him, benign and calm, like some horrible unholy thing.

"Melody, please!"

But the smile faded, and the thing before him opened its mouth. And the mouth kept screaming.

MONOCHROME DANCERS

As a girl, Mrs Tate read fairy tales where a beautiful and wise queen would only have to imagine her most perfect child for them to materialise in her arms. There was no ugliness of coupling with a man, only the desire to be a mother.

Of course, Mrs Tate grew up to the reality that life was no fairy tale. To conceive a child, she would need to debase herself with a man, rutting like a filthy animal. That was something she had no interest in. So, she devoted herself to her career instead. She worked for forty years as a formidable secretary to the CEO of a company that manufactured drills. She never married but eventually grew out of 'Miss Tate' and started to go by 'Mrs' anyway. Her back sloped, her face grew lined and hard, and her already gruff and blunt way of speaking became more so.

Eventually, she retired and withdrew to her childhood home to relax and enjoy her golden years in peace.

Without the hustle and bustle of an 8-5, Mrs Tate found herself thinking of those children, the ones she could not, in the end, wish into reality like some wonderful but ultimately doomed fairy tale queen.

There were always two children, a boy and a girl. Having spent most of her adolescence as an only child, Mrs Tate believed that a child should always have a friend to play with on those dull, rainy days. She imagined them as a little boy and girl, no more than five or six years old. They were both beautiful, big-eyed, and smiling like two china dolls. Babies never appealed to Mrs Tate; she found their scrunched up faces to be the ugliest things she had ever seen. Her children would never be grotesque like that.

The boy was light whilst the girl was dark. His hair was so blonde it almost seemed white, and his big dark eyes always sparkled. The girl had thick black hair that trailed down to her waist. Mrs Tate would braid it for her, humming like her mother had. With their pale skin and matching smiles, the children were like a black and white copy of each other.

Mrs Tate thought of them often and as fondly as if she had borne them. The three of them would play Grandma's Footsteps together and make shadow puppets on the walls at night. Her so-called golden years were dull, but her children brought her some joy, some excitement.

She could have tried to adopt, but the truth of the matter was, real children, real motherhood, did not appeal to her in the least. If one sat beside her on the bus into the city, she would scowl and glare. If one brushed past her whilst playing some inane game, she would wipe away the infected area as if cleaning off slime. On her last day at work, she met the pretty, vapid young thing who replaced her. The silly girl asked if she was 'spending her retirement looking after her grandchildren.' To which Mrs Tate coldly informed her that she found children utterly deplorable, and the need to procreate, a sign of weakness and vanity.

Her way of speaking had always cost Mrs Tate her company. She found her true friends in novels or in her imagination. Real people were rude and flawed and could not be counted on. She was, in truth, an utterly solitary creature, you might pity her, but she would not thank you for it. She was the terror of her church, as she despised people she deemed false or simpering. She went to the community centre a street from her home every Thursday to play bridge. This was mostly to avoid people thinking of her as odd. The other elderly women she played with irritated her to no end. She referred to them as 'drippy old bags' to anyone who asked, sneered at their bouncy white curls and polished nails. Who did they think they were fooling?

Mrs Tate did not need a community of her peers. For her, her imaginary children were enough.

The children lived beneath her house. The basement had been converted into a bomb shelter by her father, who feared their country being destroyed from above. At the height of his anxiety, he had converted the old-fashioned basement into something he believed would withstand an air raid.

Although her father died in France, the enemy never did attack their little town. The bomb shelter became a fortified underground study that Mrs Tate and her mother had filled with her father's books.

Every day at 4pm, Mrs Tate would descend the steps, unlock the door, wrestle with the manual wheel that kept the steel shelter sealed up and step in amongst the books and games. Her father's desk became her desk, his comfy red armchair became her red armchair, and all was well. At ten minutes past four, like clockwork, her two precious children would appear. They would slope in as if popping up from out of the ground.

Always tied together at the wrist with blood-red string. They would float, long limbs gliding, twirling like they were caught in some elegant dance.

They never spoke, Mrs Tate was raised to believe that children should be seen and not heard, so she didn't mind that. There was no intelligence in mindless chatter.

As they finished their dance, the two of them would settle at her feet, bright eyes staring up at her, smiling. She would feed them sweets, read them stories. She wouldn't touch them; she was sure that would shatter the illusion. It would make them leave.

The two of them only existed down in the basement. The boy and girl always together, always happy to see her. If anyone got wind of it, they would think she was crazy. Words would start getting tossed around, cruel and ill-informed labels like 'dementia' or 'senile' or 'mad.' Her mind was as sharp as a knife. Those old biddies at the bridge club were the ones who needed their heads examined. They could scarcely remember what day it was, let alone anything important like how to take care of themselves.

"It must be ever so lonely for you, Agnes," Mrs Battersby said in her high simpering voice. She was in an unfortunate habit of tilting her head to the side when she was about to say something particularly stupid. "No grandchildren to visit. I don't know how I'd get by without my boys."

"No," Mrs Tate said. "I am quite content. Thank you."

"That's Agnes for you," said Mrs Cottlepot. "Our independent."

Mrs Tate doubted that Mrs Cottlepot knew the meaning of the word 'independent.' She moved from her childhood home to her husband's, to her daughter's.

She would grit her teeth and withstand their company. You have to allow yourself some socialisation. People talk otherwise. It's all people are good for. The only thing you could ever count on them to do.

In all honesty, bridge bored her immensely. But one can't spend all one's time in a bunker with imaginary children. After going through the tedium of socialising, she would feel like she had earned her time at home, in the bunker, amongst the smell of old books with the children.

The bunker had always felt homelier than the house. She would even find herself humming as she descended the stairs, humming being something she usually loathed. Opening the steel door, her face wrinkled into a smile as she called, "My darlings, I'm back!"

This time only the Girl emerged from nowhere, slanting on her left ever so slightly as she tried to dance alone, bobbing and swaying. She twirled into the empty space where the Boy would usually be, out of routine.

"Where is the Boy?" Mrs Tate asked.

The Girl did not answer. She only replied in the tiny, tickling giggle that the two of them spoke in.

"No, no, you answer me properly," Mrs Tate said firmly. "Where is the Boy?"

The Girl giggled again, stumbling as she twirled, this time falling to the ground with a thud. Mrs Tate's joints ached as she bent down, still not daring to touch her.

"Girl? Girl, where is he?"

She looked up at her and started to shake her head, laughing and laughing. Tears brimmed in her eyes and streamed down her cheeks as she continued to shake her head. Then from behind the bookshelf, Mrs Tate spotted the Boy. He was curled up on the floor, coughing. A greenish vomit splattered on the carpet in front of him, he rasped, coughing hard.

Her whole body twisted in revulsion. Backing away from the Girl, she pointed accusingly at them.

"Stop that!" she snapped. "Stop that! This isn't supposed to—what's wrong with you?"

Still giggling, the Girl swayed over to the Boy, where she sat, softly patting his head. Mrs Tate ran from the bunker, sealing it up. She sat, panting on the stairs, catching her breath. After ten minutes, she went back inside, hoping the bizarre fantasy was over and she would find the two of them to be the same sweet, smiling children they always were.

The door opened, and the Girl was stood right in front of the entrance. She was laughing loudly, small black teeth on display, laughing with arms outstretched to her. The Boy lay on the ground in the centre of the room, grunting as he vomited onto the carpet. It was not a pretty red ribbon that bound them together now, but a thick rope that burnt and reddened the skin around their wrists.

Mrs Tate slammed the door behind her and ran up the stairs.

She left the house, frantically pulling on her coat. She needed to buy medicine. The Boy needed medicine urgently. She was at the door of her local pharmacy when her body froze. Mrs

Rasheed, the pharmacist, would ask her why she was buying children's medicine. She would ask, and Mrs Tate would lie. Mrs Rasheed would know. She knew she was single, childless, friendless ...

They would say that she had lost her mind. People would come. They would come and butt their noses in where they didn't belong.

Mrs Tate caught a bus into the city. She went to a supermarket and bought the children's medicine from a bored teenager with garish green hair and a nose ring—the world seemed such a frightening place now.

"Grandchildren sick?" The teenager asked.

"Yes, poor thing. He's with his mother at home."

The lie came quickly as though she had said it time after time before.

The girl cast the medicine inside the plastic bag without looking, without any further questions.

The medicine was tossed into the bunker, and Mrs Tate waited outside, trembling and anxious. It felt like hours, but then she heard the two of them laughing. It was just a bad dream. A worry that manifested into an upsetting spectacle.

But then, at their next storytime, Mrs Tate found that green sticky vomit caked into the carpet. The children danced around her as she scrubbed. Colour returned to the Boy's cheeks, and he kissed hers when she offered it to him. It was the most physical contact she could stand.

And that was the end of the whole ugly matter.

*

Mrs Tate had always been a big-boned woman. She looked foolish in pretty dresses and comical when she danced. Her girlfriends from work flocked to dances with the young men. A younger Mrs Tate would have been dragged along, sat in the corner, scowling at any man who pitied her enough to ask for a dance, strongly wishing to be anywhere else in the world.

With no beauty in the act, it was utterly pointless.

It surprised her, the joy she felt as she watched the children dance. There was no gender to their movements, no man to lead or woman to follow, no dirty grabbing or bucking of the hips like a beast. The two of them twirled, elegant as ballerinas, moves that matched their gentle hand-holding and light and flowing footwork.

There was a purity in their every step that ensnared her.

The children inherited her dislike for touching. They wouldn't cling to her. Even if she offered it out of a fictitious maternal guilt, both of them would shy away from her.

*

One cold October day, Mrs Tate came down to the basement to find the two of them already waiting for her, stood very close to the door.

"What are you two doing?" she asked, taken aback.

They wouldn't meet her eyes. They stepped back and made to begin their dance.

"No," Mrs Tate snapped. "What were you doing by the door?"

Giggling anxiously, the Boy brought two hairpins out from behind his back. The Girl began to laugh as well, her whole body shaking from exertion.

"You were trying to go outside?" she asked.

The Boy nodded, but the Girl just kept laughing.

"Hand those to me."

He did so, wide dark eyes crinkled from laughter.

"The two of you want to leave the shelter?"

At their nod, Mrs Tate's heart softened. The two of them could never go outside; they could never leave this room. Even if the children were to leave the shelter, they would get to know the house, and like the shelter, they would tire of it. They would ask to go outside.

Outside was impossible. Tears brimmed in her eyes, and Mrs Tate put her hands on their shoulders.

"I'm sorry," she said. "You must stay in here."

She took the pins from the Boy's hand and put them in her pocket. The children nodded, both still giggling as tears rolled down their cheeks, pooling under identical pale chins.

Children could get the strangest notions.

*

Her dreams were always violent and consuming. It had been that way since she was young. Often, she wondered if it was reflective of the era in which she grew up. Although, thinking on it, the old dears from bridge couldn't fathom an intelligent thought, let alone a violent one.

Perhaps intelligence factored into it. An intelligent woman, her age, working as a secretary to that tiresome oaf and then his disgusting son for her entire professional life, was bound to harbour some resentments. And before that, her brilliant father going to war and leaving her with her hysterical mother. It did not make for a calm mind.

There were two surviving pictures of the Tate's. A before and after.

The first was taken before. Her father, Mr Tate, was an enthusiastic librarian. He was the centre of the family. You could see it in the picture. Broad-shouldered with short dark hair and a curling moustache. He had his arm around his slender, bug-eyed wife. Her wispy blonde hair tied back, and she smiled with a hesitation in her eyes as if she were doing something she shouldn't. Beside them, a young boy and a girl, Lucas and Agnes.

The boy was slender and dark-haired with wide eyes and an easy smile that was the most natural thing in the world for him. The girl was tall and stocky, just as dark, with small eyes and an uncomfortable smile as if it did not come naturally to her even when she was happy.

A family before the war.

The second was taken after the conflict ended. Mr Tate and

his intelligent mind and curling moustache lay at the bottom of the sea in a boat that had been blown to pieces. Only Mrs Tate remained, pale and gaunt, her hair bedraggled, her face skull-like with eyes that bulged out of her head like her brain had swollen. She smiled wide, hysteria now plastered over her face where it was once hidden by caution. Caution destroyed by loss.

Beside her was one child where two had been before. Both had been sent away to the countryside for safety, and yet only one returned. A tall and stocky girl with small distrusting eyes and the stiff, tight-lipped smile she would wear for the rest of her life.

The violent dreams came when she and her mother were alone. The then Miss Tate would spend her days quiet and obedient. She would escape her mother and curl up in her father's armchair. She would read away reality. Bear meals of forced silence or her mother's hissed rantings and ravings. She would clean up messes of smashed glasses and plates. Clean up tears and self-inflicted cuts from her mother's trembling form.

Her mother's temper embarrassed her. There was something base and savage about it.

Still, when Mrs Tate went to bed, baseness and savagery ruled her.

Beast-like, she would stalk through the trenches, tearing the enemy men apart with her bare hands. When all the men were vanquished, she—the Beast—would fly to Britain. She would find the man who never went to war with the others, the man who came in the night to her mother and took a great many things.

The Beast would rip his body to pieces, eat the offending item first, so he knew real terror before cutting away his flesh and swallowing him whole.

Next, the Beast would travel to the countryside. The Beast would find the farm that two children were sent to for sanctuary as bombs fell down from the sky like rain. The Beast would find the little boy sick in his bed and lick his wounds to heal the infection. The Beast would tell the boy's cowardly older sister that it would all be well.

And then the Beast would eat Mrs Mills, the farmer. He would whip her first with her husband's belt, so she knew the suffering she had inflicted on those she'd promised to protect. The Beast would bite off her head and let her screaming reside inside forevermore.

Life could be however you needed it to be when you slept.

*

Her mother and Miss Tate stayed in that house, sleeping on top of the bomb shelter study. Miss Tate became Mr Stoke's secretary. Her life followed regulations and social rules. Stocky and plain, she never had trouble from men. Plain women are patronised but generally allowed to get along with whatever mundane task has been assigned to them.

Do it for long enough, and you become essential.

Obedient and dull by day, but at night while Miss Tate slept, the Beast rampaged. First, the Beast would eat the fearful elderly Mrs Tate, so she could no longer hurt herself or others. Afterwards, it would desecrate the house, pulling the walls down, leaving only the bomb shelter untouched.

Next, it would head into the city, destroying indiscriminately. It would eat the rude and judgmental postman, tear off the limbs of the sneering dolly birds at the bus stop like the insects they were. It would go into the office and rip Miss Tate's well-organised filing cabinets from the walls. It would snap her desk in half, break the telephone into a thousand pieces. The Beast would bite Mr Stoke and his laughing colleagues, let them bleed out like pigs.

The Beast would—

The violence always ended suddenly, and she was Miss Tate again. She would get out of bed, make breakfast for herself and her mother. She would endure some snarky remark from the postman. She would stand alongside the dolly birds at the bus stop, ignore their teasing about her clothes. She would pay a higher fare to use the bus than the pretty women who flirted with the red-nosed driver.

She would go to the office and perform whatever mundane task was expected of her. She would keep her boss's affairs in order. And when the day was done, she would return home to find her mother scratching or cleaning or scrubbing due to some new anxiety. Miss Tate would make them dinner and put her mother to bed before settling down herself.

The cycle of violence would begin again, and life went on.

Her children couldn't grow up in a world like that. It wasn't safe.

*

There were mornings she awoke, even now, tormented by the actions of her dreams. Though retired from her days as a secretary, the Beast still found cause to rage.

The old biddies from bridge were ripped apart over and over again. The church hall ransacked, the windows smashed. Ugly hats and tartan scarves left amongst the entrails.

The Beast would wreck the house again and again before finally descending down to the shelter. Her darlings stood no chance against the Beast. He would pull them to him with the chains around their feet. He would rip out the Girls' tongue first and then the Boy's so they could not scream. He would roar down at them, beat them brutally, claw at their bodies, scratch them, throw them against the walls.

Sometimes the Beast would leave them sobbing. At others, they would lie quiet, naked and bloody from the floggings.

Mrs Tate would awaken, petrified, only to find her children the same sweet and gentle creatures they always were.

Dreams were only that, just dreams and nothing more.

*

It was a Sunday. The vicar had helped her home after a funny turn. Already embarrassed, Mrs Tate had invited him in for a slice of coffee cake. It was more than her mother would have done. Her mother had grown too frightened of men to leave the house. She had burst into tears when the former vicar, Minister Fanton, had visited the place. Even a holy man could not be trusted.

Mrs Tate had passed the vicar a cup of tea to go with the thin slice of cake. He was blathering on about something or other, attempting to get her to help out with some fundraiser. Rich of him to ask that of an elderly woman he had only just finished walking home.

Over her shoulder, Mrs Tate spotted a familiar figure at the top of the stairs. Her heart flew to her throat. The Girl was stood on the top step, arm dwindling on the bannister, peering down at them curiously.

"Do excuse me, Father," Mrs Tate said swiftly, getting to her feet. "I must pop upstairs."

Fortunately, the young man stayed seated. Mrs Tate ascended the stairs, the Girl dashed along the hallway. Praying she would not giggle, that she would not make a sound, Mrs Tate caught her by one skinny arm as she attempted to pass her. Clamping a hand over the Girl's mouth, Mrs Tate bundled her into the linen closet in the bedroom.

Panic rose in her chest as she moved a chair in front of the door. How had she gotten out? And if she had—where was the Boy? The red string that bound them together was nowhere to be seen.

It was hard to disguise the fear on her face as she returned downstairs. The Boy seemed to appear out of the corner of her eye while that clueless young vicar washed down his cake. The second he was out the door, still insisting that she call to let him know if she changed her mind about the fundraiser, Mrs Tate dashed upstairs.

The Girl was sat amongst the linen, a bored expression on her face.

"How did you get out here?" Mrs Tate demanded.

The Girl giggled.

"No. You answer me now!"

Again she laughed. Mrs Tate hauled her to her feet and marched her downstairs. The shelter door was swung open all the way, to her horror. Mrs Tate's heart flew to her mouth. She pushed the Girl inside.

"Boy! Boy! Where are you?"

The Boy stepped out from behind a bookshelf. He giggled and waved.

The Girl rushed to him and clasped his hands in hers, both of them laughing together.

I must be mad, Mrs Tate thought as she covered her mouth with her hands. I must be mad.

*

The shelter was locked, and Mrs Tate avoided it. She would leave food through the flap. Madness. When she felt ready to return, she would have to clear up piles of rotting food. Yet, she couldn't bear the thought of them starving.

It wasn't good for her to be down there. Not now.

It was best to forget them, to put all this behind her as much as it would hurt. She would let them sleep.

She was becoming like Mother, hysterical. Mother, who had been so afraid of children that she would have rejected her own, had he returned. For all her love, Mrs Tate knew that was not the way to be.

Life was dull. Those bridge bags didn't do much in terms of company. Old men repulsed her even more, self-satisfied, selfish, confused, thought they knew it all. They were bad when they were young, and now they were even worse.

No companionship for the elderly. Flat-eyed children coming to read to them, barely able to spit out what was right in front of them. Life was unbearably boring in her old age. Mrs Tate found herself thinking of the shelter often. Of Boy and Girl and their sweet laughter.

Her dreams had become violent again. The two children

were chained to each other at the ankles and wrists. The tunics they wore were sodden with urine and sweat. The floor was stained with blood and faeces. The stench reeked like death and hung over her father's books.

The children would try to run as the Beast came down upon them, bruising and beating. The Beast didn't tear or rip or maim as he did in the other dreams. Faces and pale pink skin, he punched and pinched until it grew dark and hard. Slaps that struck again and again and again and again and again.

The Boy bled so very much as the Girl tried to run, dragging his unconscious body behind her.

The Beast grabbed her head and wrenched her down onto the ground. He got on top of her and forced her eyes open as he screamed in her face. Her eyes wrinkled up, and she sobbed from her tongueless mouth.

It was so vile and so strange that when the Beast howled, he and Mrs Tate sounded almost exactly alike.

Mrs Tate would awaken in a cold sweat and tell herself over and over that dreams were only dreams. Hysteria was a plague, and no good would come from abiding it. She wanted desperately to check on the children, but even in their beauty, they fed into the ugliness of her mind.

There was no need to check on children who did not exist. The nightmares would fade into something good, something positive, and Mrs Tate would feel better. That was what she told herself on those mornings when her hands wouldn't stop shaking.

*

One night she wandered down to the shelter to get a book. Her hand on the lock, she found herself unable to open it. Her chest ached, Mrs Tate sat down on the stairs, facing the door. Her knees creaked unceremoniously, and she let out a sigh.

"I don't know if the two of you can hear me," she said. "I don't know my own mind sometimes. But, if you are there and you are listening, would you like to hear a story?"

Silence. She thought that in the distance, there was a giggle. No—that was her imagination. Her hands clenched, bunching the material of her skirt.

No matter. This story was better told to no-one than heard by the innocent.

"This is a story from a long time ago; the world was a different place. I don't suppose the two of you know about the war. I never wanted you to know about horrible things like that. But . . . that's where it begins."

Silence. No laughter, no giggling, no tapping of dancing feet. Feeling truly alone, Mrs Tate took a deep breath.

*

"Once upon a time, there was a young girl and her brother. The two of them had an incredibly happy life. Their mother was kind and beautiful, and their father was a scholar. Life was good. The family would take holidays to the seaside and long walks in the park. They were always together. The girl, despite all the joy in her life, was quiet and sullen. Her brother, on the other hand, was a delightful child who charmed everyone he met. Though they were very different, the two of them loved each other very much.

Their charmed life came to an end when the boy was nine years old. A great war broke out over Europe, and all the men left to fight. The children's father went away and died within a year. He drowned when the ship he worked on was sunk by German submarines. Their mother fell into despair and finally agreed with the nosey women from church to send the girl and her brother away to the countryside.

She promised them that they would be safe from the bombing and danger out there. She said it would be like an adventure. She told the boy to listen to his sister and told the girl to protect her brother. The girl saw her mother dissolve into tears as the train set off, carrying them far from home.

The countryside impressed the girl less than the city had. Fields and fields for miles until the train finally stopped in a little northern town. Her brother smiled the whole time like he refused to let their misfortune hurt him.

A woman with very thick glasses met them from the train and drove them to a farmhouse just a stone's throw from the village. Their caretaker during the evacuation was a woman named Moira Mills. She was stern with untidy short hair and permanently smoked a pipe. She smiled once whilst the woman with glasses was still there.

She asked them if they were good, hard-working children and gave a disbelieving hum when the girl mumbled that they were.

Mrs Mills's husband and two grown-up sons had gone to war, leaving her with a small farm to run. For a woman, she was incredibly strong and could lift a barrel of hay upon her shoulder. The girl and boy were put to work quickly. The rules here were that if you did not work, you did not eat. Food was scarce, and Mrs Mills kept the majority of it for herself.

It was the first time in her life that her brother had failed to charm an adult. In fact, Mrs Mills took an exceptional and immediate dislike to the little boy.

Whereas the girl found it easy to switch off and get along with any menial task, her brother had never been treated harshly before. He struggled, stumbled and got upset easily. The two of them had been there for two days when her brother managed to evoke Mrs Mills's wrath.

He had been playing in the chicken coup instead of collecting eggs.

Mrs Mills had seized him and beaten him with a man's belt.

Her brother had never been beaten, never had an adult raise a hand to him his whole life. The violence of the act terrified both of them. Playing in the chicken coup was the last time the girl ever saw her brother smile.

Their time together after that was very lonely. Lost to desperation and fear, the children kept their heads down, strived to get by. Mrs Mills drank and raged. Seeing how they feared the belt, she began to use it as a threat—'Have this done by noon or you'll get the belt.' Spilling food, wasting water, making a mess, making a sound, would get you the belt, or sometimes you would go without food.

It happened less to the girl than it did her brother, whom Mrs Mills harboured a burning dislike. She would hide objects around the house and demand that he find them quickly. The girl would listen to her little brother weeping in his sleep, terrified of the morning ahead. They would whisper to each other of running away, but the girl knew it was impossible.

Mrs Mills had the power, the threat of something worse looming over them.

All the while, the girl was consumed with guilt. She had to protect her brother, and she couldn't. She would obediently sweep the yard while Mrs Mills whipped him bloody. She would avert her eyes when she saw the stinging welts on his back as he changed. She would hold his hand and do nothing.

Protecting her beloved brother from an adult was not something she could do.

The bad thing happened three months into their evacuation. Her brother had grown very attached to a horse and had been stealing apples to feed it. She had warned him to stop, that Mrs Mills would catch him and punish him worse than she ever had before.

It wasn't enough to deter her brother. And as she had warned, he was caught.

This time, the belt was kept aside. Its absence was somehow much more devastating. Her brother was left awaiting some terrible beating, not knowing when it would come.

He was denied meals, denied his bed, even denied access back into the house. When it began to rain, Mrs Mills locked the door and watched him out there in the yard like an animal. The girl was locked in her room all night, so she couldn't let him in.

The girl would never forget the way the rain and wind raged

against the window. She tried to plead with Mrs Mills, who stated coldly that if the boy wanted to waste food on an animal he should join them.

The bad night passed, and the next morning, her brother was allowed back inside for breakfast. His hands trembled, and his eyes were heavy in his skull.

He said in a tiny voice that he had learned his lesson.

The girl found him collapsed in the chicken coup that afternoon. His little body burned, and yet he shivered and complained that he was ever so cold.

When the doctor was called, Mrs Mills didn't mention that she had made a little boy in her care sleep outside in the pouring rain. She said that city children had a poor constitution.

The doctor didn't stay for long. When he came out, he put his hand on the girl's arm and told her he was sorry. It was what everyone said to her when her father died as well. The girl and Mrs Mills went through the rest of the war with the little boy's ghost between them.

Eventually, the war ended, and the young girl was allowed to return home to her mother. Tragically, however, her mother was a much-changed woman. Driven mad by grief, she could not stand the loss of her son. Living alone amongst the air raids, her mother had suffered further at the hands of a man who left her terrified of all those like him. The girl was made to stay at her side, away from boys, away from men who may do them harm.

The neighbours stopped calling on them. Nobody dared ask about the son, who lay buried in a grave so far away from home. It was less painful for her mother that way. It was like he never existed. It was almost painless that way. Yes, almost as if it didn't even matter."

*

Mrs Tate wiped a tear from her eye.

"You children can't imagine how toxic it was to come home to her like that. To live my life without comfort from anyone."

She held her face in her hands. "And now, children, I am afraid that I'm losing my mind. Everything is stretched and pulled together too hard. I don't even . . ." She took a breath. "If you're really there, please show me a sign."

Tap-Tap-Tap.

And Mrs Tate's sobs turned to screams.

*

For, of course, there was another story. One she had bid herself to forget as it was too painful, too shameful for her to entertain. It is their story as well as hers, and if they had the means to do so, they would tell it to you.

This is a story you might know, in part, from the news.

A six-year-old boy was taken from a park while his mother went to clean up his baby brother. The police searched and searched, but the child was never found. A month later, an eight-year-old girl was taken. She had been on a school trip with her class and never came back from the toilets. A great deal of blood was found in the woods nearby, but no body.

You might have seen the faces of those two children staring out at you from walls and lamp posts—a little boy with pale blonde hair and big dark eyes. And a girl with silky black hair and scowling blue eyes.

The two of them lived in a bomb shelter under the house of an old woman, unable to scream or cry for help or even communicate with one another, for the creature they knew as the 'Beast' had removed their tongues. Bound together at the ankles and wrists, the two children dreamt of escape.

Their captor had two personas. The old woman who came and read to them. She could not see the bruises, the bites, the blood, and the ropes. She couldn't see their soiled clothes or their blackened teeth. She read them stories and brought them sweets.

Then there was the Beast. He came, naked and withered into the shelter. He would snarl and bite, scratch, kick and beat. He would leave, hissing before the morning came. He would leave the shelter door unlocked, knowing they would not go, even if they could break free of their chains.

*

Mrs Tate pushed open the unlocked door, and there they were. The smell—how could she have ignored it? The smell of faeces, blood, vomit, and sweets. The children, her two precious dancing angels, sat in chains, staring at her through beaten, purpled eyes.

She howled, covering her face with her hands, staggering backwards. Her heart smashed against her chest and echoed like the clanging of bells in her ears.

There was no Beast. It had been her own hands who made those bruises, who locked them in chains. It had been her who raged every night. It had been her who took them from outside and brought them down here.

They weren't sweet smiling dolls. Boy was tall and gaunt, with huge dark eyes that filled his pale head like a skull and white hair that hung down past his shoulders like feathers. The Girl was the same, her eyes wide and unblinking. Her black hair matted into dark, limp braids.

The thrashing, the blood, the terrible grunting sound her voiceless mouth had made.

"What have I done? What have I done to you?" Mrs Tate wept, reaching a hand towards them. The two of them cowered back like her touch would kill them. The Girl crouched protectively over the Boy.

"I couldn't have—this can't be real. . . ." She covered her face with her hands, clamping them over her eyes again and again. Each time they were there, pressed to the wall, moaning, bruised, and dreadful. She screamed and beat her hands against her face.

The children danced around her, ribbon chains clanking as they swayed. They changed, as they danced, the Boy became her brother, who lost the chance to grow up and be a man. The Girl became her, young and powerless to protect anyone.

In the middle, she became the Beast or Mrs Mills, someone wicked and damned who screamed and screamed and screamed.

Mrs Tate pushed the two of them aside, tripping on the chains, her aching knees bashed into the ground. She wept in pain, her glasses askew. The children giggled, blackened teeth grinding together. She staggered from the room, gagging on the smell, on her hands and knees as she ascended. Small hands with bloodied, broken fingernails scraped at her hair, chains rattled on the ground. Her wig was ripped off. Hands yanked at her blouse, shaking her violently.

She couldn't look—She couldn't bear to see them. Her own sobs raged in her chest. Too awake, too shocked to call upon the Beast.

The little boy had come willingly. He was bored and delighted when she offered to buy him an ice cream. He didn't even know to be afraid until he finished his rice pudding at her dinner table and realised she wasn't going to let him leave.

He raked his nails down her face, spluttering garbled, tongue-less nonsense.

The girl had approached her in the women's public bathroom of a museum. She had asked her quite boldly if everyone got so ugly when they got old. She had laughed like she was clever. The girl knew to be afraid early.

She kicked her hard between the legs, hissing through black teeth. Mrs Tate lay on her back on the stairs, shielding her face and weeping. The monochrome dancers twirled together, kicking and snarling and spitting. Her glasses cracked. Red seeped into her vision.

Pretty colours, she thought. Black and white and red.

Boy and Girl stepped over the old woman's broken body. Staggering on chains and missing toes, they made their way up the stairs. They wobbled through the living room, and then, hand in hand, they opened the front door and stepped out into the sun.

WHO IS YOUR DADDY, AND WHAT DOES HE DO?

Some Daddies are policemen or salary-men or dancing-men or professor-men or doctor-men or firemen. Some Daddies are stay-at-home-men. Of this, Claire found that hers was one of the latter. Her friend Lizzie's Daddy, had lost his job. He stayed at home on the sofa, watching auction shows on TV and looking for new jobs online.

But even he came to Parent's Evening in his well-worn brown suit and damaged grey glasses. It was only Claire's Mummy, who came every year. Though Mrs Heal, her teacher, never remembered. Every year it was always the same, "Oh Claire, did your mother come last night? I can't quite . . ."

"Daddy would love to come," Mummy would always say. "But he doesn't like crowds. I tell him all the nice things your teachers say. He knows how well you're doing. Daddy is proud of you."

That seemed fair enough. Claire didn't like crowds either. And she didn't think her Daddy even owned a suit like Lizzie's unemployed Daddy did. No, Claire's Daddy lounged around in tracksuit bottoms and comfy looking jumpers. He bit his nails, even though he was a grown-up. And his face was young, but he had pretty white hair like snow.

She didn't want her friends to think she was odd or for Mrs Heal to look at him funny. Unlike her Mummy, who always spoke directly, who couldn't be denied, Daddy babbled to himself, sang songs or recited lines from plays Claire had never seen. Sometimes he stared right through her, and at others, he seemed so lonely it was like his world would end if she left the room.

He wasn't allowed to touch her. Claire had seen films where Daddies carried their kids on their shoulders, or cuddled them in their arms, or played catch.

Claire once snuck a tennis ball down to Daddy's room in hopes that they could play catch. But he didn't really understand. The ball hit his chest, and he just stared at it on the ground.

"No, Daddy, that isn't how you play. You have to pick it up."

She had gone to reach her hand through the bars to retrieve the ball and try again.

Putting your hands through the bars isn't allowed either. Mummy came running in and yanked Claire to her feet so hard that she scraped her knees on the floor.

"You do not put your hands through the bars! You know that!" Mummy yelled.

Mummy's shouting voice made Claire cry. It made Daddy cover his ears with his hands and rock back and forth.

"I'm sorry! I was trying to play with Daddy!"

"You don't touch the bars, Claire. You could have been hurt!"

"Daddy wouldn't hurt me!"

He had been reaching for her with shaking pale hands and bloody broken nails.

"Yes! He would have! Don't be so stupid."

Claire covered her ears too and began to cry even louder. At this, her mother softened. She bent down and pulled her into her arms.

"I'm sorry I shouted at you," she said. "I put rules in place to protect you and to protect Daddy, Claire. It would break his heart if he hurt you by accident."

"Other kids get to play catch!" Claire wailed.

"I'm sorry," she said. "Daddy loves you. He's just a little different. We're a little different as a family. Daddy sleeps in his room down here, behind the bars, to keep you safe."

Daddy was muttering hurriedly to himself, eyes wild and frantic. He was biting his lip again, bloody, like lipstick.

"Do you understand?"

"Yes, Mummy."

Lizzie's Daddy was called Robert. He said that Claire could call him 'Robert' when she went over for dinner.

Claire didn't know her Daddy's name for a long time. Mummy's name was short, but nobody could remember it no matter how many times Claire told them. It was like they just hadn't heard it.

She found out Daddy's name from a poster. She was walking home from Imogen's house when she saw Daddy's eye through a gap between some papers on a lamppost. She pulled down the lost cat, the rock band poster, and the flier about raising money for the town centre. She pulled away the ad about the garden centre opening on the outskirts of town.

There was Daddy. Or . . . it looked like Daddy. His hair was chestnut brown and wavy. He wasn't pale, and he had a huge smile. It lit up the brown eyes that Claire was used to seeing buzzing and blank.

Claire could read pretty well for her age. Mummy taught her before she started school. The poster said 'Missing' and the name 'Nick Andrews.' But that didn't make sense. Daddy wasn't missing at all, he was at home, he was in his room with the bars that kept her safe. If people saw this poster, they might think that . . .

She ripped the poster down and wedged it between the pages of her handwriting book. Best to keep it hidden. It might hurt Daddy's feelings if he saw it. He might be embarrassed. Mummy didn't like pictures of herself either.

Not that she'd show Mummy the poster. This felt private, something that was just for Claire.

She frowned over her homework again.

'Who is your Daddy, and What Does He Do?'

She nibbled on her blue crayon. She had contemplated drawing Daddy in his room, but the other kids would think that he was a bad man in prison. She thought about drawing Daddy eating, but Mummy said that their food was a secret. People wouldn't understand. They might ask questions. Mummy hated questions. She got mad if Claire asked her things.

Who is Your Daddy?

That part was easy. He was Nick Andrews.

But Claire didn't know anything else. People thought he went missing at age nineteen, but he didn't at all. He moved in with Mummy because they were in love and they had her together. He was happy.

Well, she thought he was happy. He didn't smile like he did in his secret missing person poster, but he usually seemed ... content in his room.

Claire unfolded the poster from its place in her handwriting book.

She put her crayon to the paper and began to draw the smiling brown-haired man in the picture. The poster said that he was a journalism student. Mummy said that journalists wrote newspapers. So Claire added a newspaper next to her drawing.

The lie was easier.

Claire put her homework in her bag and skipped downstairs.

"Dinner is nearly ready," Mummy warned as Claire opened the basement door.

"I'm just going to play with Daddy for a few minutes."

Mummy laughed. "Well, alright, but be quick. And no playing catch, okay?"

"Okay!" Claire called.

Daddy was different from how he was in the poster, to other Daddies like Lizzie's, but he was hers. That was good enough.

Fini

ACKNOWLEDGEMENTS

This collection paints a pretty dark picture of humans in general, so here's some good people whose support keeps me going:

Amanda, Kate, Meg, and Emily, who read bits from this collection at a first draft. My brother, Ieuan, my parents, Lesley and Paul, and my sister, Charlotte, and her partner Andy. My in-laws, Joy, Ian and Mili. My CU crew, Nav, Elise, Carly, Gary and Daniel. My friends, Anwen, Niamh and Pearl. As well as my grandparents, who definitely shouldn't read a single word of this, and my Uncle Stephen, for always being there to chat about books. Carly Holmes, for her support with this project; you're an icon!

I'd also like to thank Alan Bilton, my PhD supervisor, for his ongoing support, as well as the department of English & Creative Writing at Swansea University.

This collection wouldn't be a reality without Tessa and the fantastic team at Bear Hill; thank you for having faith in my grisly little collection.

And finally, George, always and forever. Thank you!

FROM THE AUTHOR

I decided to write *Human Beings* initially as an exercise in exploring the darker side of human nature, negotiating the apparently normal spaces of human lives while retaining the violent and vile acts that exist within them. As a result of this, the collection blossomed into a series of portraits of individuals and their motivations to damage themselves and others. The intended result of this endeavour is to tell stories without compromise that use their sometimes disturbing imagery to haunt the reader long after the book has been set back to its shelf-slumber.

Rachael Llewellyn is an English novelist. Her previous work includes the Red Creek series (*Down Red Creek* and *Impulse Control*, both with Sulis International Press), and her short fiction has appeared in numerous anthologies and journals. She is currently a PhD candidate at Swansea University, and is completing her thesis on trauma and memory in folklore.

Find Rachael of Twitter @FumigatedSpace

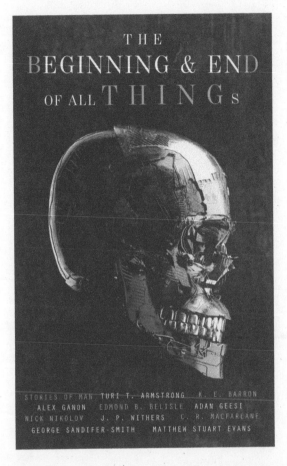

9 781989 071311